The Gelignite
Gang

The Gelignite Gang

John Creasey

PERENNIAL LIBRARY

Harper & Row, Publishers, New York
Cambridge, Philadelphia, San Francisco, Washington
London, Mexico City, São Paulo, Singapore, Sydney

PR
6053
R3
I48
1987

A hardcover edition of this book was originally published in England under the title *Inspector West Makes Haste*. A hardcover edition of *The Gelignite Gang* was published in the United States in 1955 by Harper & Brothers.

First PERENNIAL LIBRARY edition published 1987.

Library of Congress Cataloging-in-Publication Data
Creasey, John.
  The gelignite gang.

  Previously published as: Inspector West makes haste. I. title.
PR6005.R517I5   1987   823'.912   87-45037
ISBN 0-06-080885-3 (pbk.)

87 88 89 90 91 OPM 10 9 8 7 6 5 4 3 2 1

1

The Robbers

The scraping noise was almost the only sound; that and hushed breathing. One of the three men kept catching his breath as if he were stifling a sneeze. Each had a set task, each carried it out. The biggest, wearing a dark brown overcoat, stood by the door of the safe, pushing the gelignite into the keyhole. The other two piled stacks of paper, records of the big department store, round the walls, to muffle the sound of the explosion. That was all.

The biggest man glanced over his shoulder and jerked his head. The smallest went across to him, rubber-soled shoes squeaking faintly on the cement floor.

"Yeh?"

"See if Billy's okay."

"Okay." The smallest man trotted back to the door, which was open just wide enough for him to pass through. In a few minutes, when Billy had given the all clear, the door would be closed, more piles of papers stacked against it, and the safe would be blown. That was the moment to pray for.

Just now, there was too much time to think, to wonder what would happen if the cops—

Outside, there was a kind of hallway. To the right and the left were heavy double doors leading to large basement storerooms. In front, opposite the so-called strongroom door, was the service lift. The open crisscross of shiny black ironwork showed the dirty, cobwebby walls, the main shaft, the loop of the cable beneath the car itself.

By the side of the lift shaft was a flight of narrow concrete steps.

The smallest man went up these hurriedly but quietly. His feet now made little slithering sounds. He reached the next floor, wooden boards, strips of brown carpet, the feet of chairs and tables, the solid bases of big showcases and more big double doors. The light was dim and shadowy, as if far away: pale imitation daylight from the display windows. By day, when the store was open, these double doors which led to the ground-floor salesrooms were kept closed. By night they were kept wide open, and some of the windows could be seen from them.

Beyond the window displays was the city of London. Dark streets, dark houses, unlit windows, still traffic, a silent, sleeping city, for this was two o'clock in the morning.

Above the light, above this man's head, were six other floors, all crammed with goods—furniture, fabrics, hats, coats, dresses, jewelry, cutlery, men's wear, junior wear, beach wear, night—oh, everything a London store would sell. Above were the two night watchmen, too. This was the time they met each night on the top floor to compare notes and to agree that all was well.

On this ground floor, a man stood by a showcase which gleamed dully.

He was very young, and just then staring toward the street outside, which ran into Oxford Street not many yards along. He made a tall, silent shape, with his back to the lift and the staircase and to the man who had just come up. He didn't move until a different light showed for a moment beyond the window.

A car passed.

There was no sound of its engine; it might have been the ghost of a car. First two bright white lights showed, then a red glow, then nothing.

The tall young man darted back as the white lights shone, then stopped and watched tensely. There was only silence, the strange shadows of the beautifully clad dummies in the windows, and the showcases.

"Billy," whispered the messenger.

The shape moved violently, the youth swung round, hands weaving, a choking noise coming from his mouth.

"Wha—" he began. "Wha—" he broke off. His breathing was twice as heavy as it had been when the messenger had first reached the floor level.

"S'only me," the messenger said casually. "What's up? Cold feet?"

"I—I thought—I thought I heard—footsteps."

"That so?" The messenger drew level with the youth, who was the taller by several inches. He gripped the youth's forearm and felt the quiver of nerve-racked muscles. He squeezed. "Listen," he said.

They listened, side by side, for at least a minute.

"Nothing," the messenger said, "forget it. Better come down, we're going to blow it."

"But—"

"Better come down." The messenger's grip on the youth's arm was very tight. "Don't you worry, Billy, everyone feels a bit queer on his first big job. You're okay. Better come down."

"But I heard—footsteps."

"Nerves," said the messenger, "just nerves, Billy. Had 'em meself. Come on."

"I tell you—"

The messenger's voice, still a whisper, acquired a different, authoritative note.

"Want me to tell the Blower you're scared?"

"No!"

"Then keep your mouth shut and come with me," hissed the messenger. His grip tightened, he twisted the other's wrist enough to propel him forward, and they went toward the stairs. Billy stumbled, making more noise than anyone had since the four robbers had broken in through the basement—from an old bombed site—an hour ago.

Billy almost fell down the stairs; would have fallen, but for the messenger's grip on his wrist. They stopped at the first half landing. When the messenger spoke again, his voice lacked the savage note of menace.

"You'll be okay, Billy. Take a nip." He slid a brandy flask out of his hip pocket. "Don't worry, I won't tell the Blower. Enough to give anyone the creeps, this is. Listen, stay right here. Give yourself a coupla minutes. I'll come back for you. Don't want the Blower to see you looking yellow as a buttercup, do you?"

"No, I— Ta." Billy gulped the brandy down, gasped, and leaned against the wall. "Thanks—

4

thanks a million. I'll be all right. But I heard—I really thought I heard those footsteps."

"That's better, you *thought*," approved the messenger. He grinned. "I'll take a looksee." He went back upstairs.

He was gone for five minutes. Billy heard no sound at all. There was just the faint light coming from the ground floor, and the silence. Then the messenger came back briskly, cockily.

"Not a sound. Them watchmen are upstairs all right," he said. "You stay, I'll tell the Blower it's okay. Okay?"

"Ye—yes, sure."

"You're doing fine." The messenger patted Billy's shoulder before going down the second flight of steps. He reached the basement, the empty lift shaft, the door which stood ajar opposite it with light streaming out. A shadow appeared, and the middle-sized man of the trio came out. He had to squeeze himself through the narrow aperture, for he had a torso like a barrel and a big, drooping stomach. In a voice which scarcely carried, he said:

"Been having a nap? He's proper mad."

"He's not so mad as he's going to be," the messenger said, and pushed past the other into the strongroom. Here, the big man who had been working at the safe stood with his hands in his overcoat pockets, the coat open and showing a suit of dark gray. This was the Blower. He looked down at the messenger, his mouth slack, his eyes narrowed, his head on one side.

"What is it?"

"It's Billy," said the messenger. "Attack of nerves," he explained laconically, and the expression of the big man's face didn't change. "So I had a look round. I didn't see anyone, I—"

A sibilant whispering sounded at the door. The big torso thrust itself forward, the door opened further, and the man beckoned. The big man, known as the Blower, and the messenger moved toward him, making no sound. They went out and pulled the door to from the outside, and the Blower locked it; keys clicked sharply.

Billy stood by the iron trelliswork of the lift, licking his lips.

Above, footsteps sounded.

The Blower switched off the light and shone a flashlight; then all three moved toward Billy. One man took Billy's wrist. They edged to one side and went through a door into a storeroom; the door was not kept locked. The broad beam of the flashlight shone on packing cases and crates, on dark, expensive furniture lining the walls, on piles of shavings and of straw, on mirrors hanging by chains from the ceiling. There was a strong smell of varnish. The flashlight showed everything, and pointed toward a part of the wall where big wardrobes stood dark against the white walls, making black depths of shadow.

"Over there," the Blower whispered.

They were close together in a bunch. The messenger had his fingers closed tightly round Billy's wrist. Billy was breathing in short, shallow gasps, and as they reached the wardrobes, the Blower said:

"Can't you keep quiet?"

Billy said, "I—" and then was seized by a spasm of shivering; his teeth chattered, he stammered one syllable. "*I-I-I-I-*" came from his lips, and he couldn't stop. "*I-I-I-I.*"

6

"Quiet!" hissed the Blower.

Billy caught his breath, and the stuttering and the chattering ceased, but the messenger could feel the youth's body quivering, knew that he would soon break down again. Yet for a moment, there was silence—except for the footsteps above.

They drew nearer. Whoever it was was coming down.

The man must have reached the foot of the steps, and be near the door. He would probably look in here. If he found anything suspicious he could do one of two things: go for the other night watchman or investigate by himself.

The footsteps were firm and deliberate, and drawing remorselessly nearer. In the storeroom there was absolute silence, tautened whenever the watchman stopped walking.

Light shone near the door, showed at the sides.

Abruptly, Billy's teeth began to chatter again; his body jumped up and down as if with ague; he just couldn't control himself. No one spoke, but the messenger raised a clenched, bony fist and smashed it into Billy's jaw. The blow jolted his head back and brought a single grunt; then silence came. The messenger stopped Billy from falling. It wasn't easy to hold him upright.

The light became brighter.

The door opened wide, and the watchman stepped inside, swinging his flashlight with quick, sweeping movements which told that he was nervous. He did not come far inside. The white light shone upon all the furniture in turn, shone into the hanging mirrors and was reflected from them brightly, filling the storeroom with shimmering, flickering brightness. Then the direction of the beam altered and the light fell on the wardrobes. The shadow there was still dark, enshrouding the silent men.

The light kept still.

There was no sound.

The night watchman coughed suddenly. The noise was like an explosion, and echoed about the big, low-ceilinged storeroom. The light wavered, then swiveled, then vanished altogether.

The door had closed on the night watchman.

The messenger breathed, "Think he guessed?"

The Blower said flatly, "After him. If he goes to a telephone, fix him. You know how."

"Okay."

"Hurry."

The man who carried the Blower's messages reached the door. His greatest asset was his ability to move while making practically no sound. He touched the door, opened it an inch, and peered outside. There was light; the night watchman's flashlight was swinging to and fro, to and fro, as he approached the stairs.

He started up, the light preceding him.

The Blower's man followed.

On the next floor the watchman put out his flashlight and moved in the light which came from the windows. Nothing stirred outside. He didn't quicken his pace, but approached a telephone which stood on a small table close to the lift car. The lift was empty and forlorn-looking in the half light.

He lifted the receiver.

The messenger from below moved.

2

The Night Watchman

While the Blower and his men were working below, Jem Maitland, one of the two night watchmen, had been thinking of his daughter....

Here, at Jefferson's, in the lonely quiet of the night, almost alone in the empty store, with the lay figures in the windows and the departments, the cold, aloof displays, the carpets, the winking glass of mirrors, of showcases and of jewelry or cutlery, he needed someone to think about. As often as not, it was Rosie.

That night he was sad; more sad than usual. He had always known that it would be inevitable, of course; Rosie was bound to want her own home sooner or later, wouldn't always be satisfied with sharing his. And now there was an "emergency." She hadn't told him yet, but what she really meant was that a baby was on the way. Maitland didn't resent the baby any more than he had resented Rosie's husband when they had married six months ago. He was just a little sorry for himself. At sixty-seven a man wanted comfort, and Rosie had given him all the comfort he could hope for. Now—well, he would manage because he would have to, although it wouldn't be the same.

But a grandchild—

That was a new, softening thought. Outside, in the little world of Brickett Street and the Mile End Road, Aldgate and Whitechapel, a thousand tiny houses looking all alike, a hundred dingy streets with a lamp post every fifty yards, ten thousand little red chimney pots above the mass of drab gray roofs, children were easily come by, whether in passion or out of boredom. Most were loved, some hated, most cared for, some neglected and abused. Maitland knew all about the children of Brickett Street, the street playground round the corner, the shouting, running, shrieking kids, dirty, unkempt and defiantly happy. In his mind's eye he could picture three families; and three mothers who pushed their babies out in spotless prams, took pride, labored with love, sewed, patched, cooked, tried hard all the time. Rosie would be like that. And he, the grandfather, would be able to help.

But a grandchild. A—grandson?

Maitland, who had left the store's other night watchman ten minutes earlier, walked down the service stairs toward the ground floor. He wasn't too happy about being here. Archer, the other man, had wanted him to stay upstairs and play dominoes for half an hour, at a bob a game. Maitland, with a stricter sense of loyalty to his employers, had said no. Archer hadn't been too pleased.

A car passed, outside; Maitland saw its lights, but there was no sound. The silence inside Jefferson's by night was uncanny; when he had first

10

taken this job on, ten years ago, he hadn't liked it at all. The big double doors and the huge, toughened glass windows made it soundproof, and every tiny sound inside was magnified—such as the ticking of the clocks in the watch-and-clock department on the first floor, and the ticking of the time clocks where he had stamped his card to show that he had been round the second, first, and ground floors according to schedule.

He had never been late for schedule yet.

Tick-tick-tick, went the time clock, *come and stamp your card. Tick-tick-tick—come-come-come.* To keep himself awake and alert, he sometimes made up words like that—as, when a small child, he had made up rhymes to the *chug-chug-chug* of train wheels.

Tonight he had plenty to keep himself alert.

Rosie wasn't showing yet, so she couldn't be far gone. Two or three months, perhaps. She hadn't liked telling him that Billy had found a small flat, just two rooms and a kitchen, in Nattur Street. Socially, that was a step up; Nattur Street houses did not debouch onto the flagstones of the pavement, but had tiny areas in front, which had been railed off before the drive for scrap iron during the war. They were lucky to get it—apparently Billy had a friend, a vague, nameless one with "influence." Well, you had to have influence to get on. Billy was all right. Jem Maitland did not particularly like him, but had no positive dislike. Billy had a lucky star, was always winning a bit on the pools, or the dogs or the horses.

He, Maitland, had never had that kind of luck. He'd been a docker during the bad years, and then injured his back. He was all right provided he didn't strain himself, carry heavy loads or run too fast. This job which Jefferson's had offered—perhaps that was his share of good fortune. Ten years, and with any luck they'd keep him on another three years until he was seventy.

By then the child would be pretty lively. Funny thing about kids, you couldn't be sure who they would take after. Rosie? Or Billy? Rosie was the quiet kind; Billy was always talking, forever asking questions. Only a few nights ago, on the way back from the pub at the corner, he'd been on about the night watchman's job here at Jefferson's. Whenever he thought of that, Maitland felt uneasy. He'd talked too freely, told Billy what schedule he had to follow, where he clocked in, where he met the other night watchman. It had been out in the open, too; anyone might have heard.

Well, they probably hadn't.

He reached the ground floor without dreaming that the Blower's man was waiting for him.

Near him were the showcases and display stands for handbags. A faint smell of leather and polish crept from them. Each department had its own smell, and Maitland could find his way about here blindfolded. Even the jewelry and silver-plate department had a smell of its own, making a kind of sharpness in the nostrils. He always disliked it. It was the only spot in the whole store where he ever felt nervous. Once, four years ago, smash-and-grab bandits had hurled a stone through the nearest window, and started to grab. Maitland had been on the ground floor on his own. Whenever he thought of it, he had the feeling which had come to him the moment he had realized that it was a raid.

Fear.

He had turned cold, shivered violently, felt his teeth gritting, and then, as the dark figures in the window had grabbed, he had made his way to the telephone, called Archer—the same watchman who was now upstairs—and then sidled toward the alarm bell. The whole store had awakened to the hideous ringing, the raiders had fled and he'd gone after them, bellowing, wholly astonished at the surge of courage. As luck would have it, police in a patrol car had been in Oxford Street and heard the alarm. The three men had gone down for two years each, and Maitland still treasured a newspaper cutting telling of the judge's praise for his prompt and courageous action.

Only Rosie knew how scared he'd been!

Rosie wasn't quite so close to him as she had been. Maitland had a feeling that she knew he was never really at ease with Billy, although they would go down to the Red Cow occasionally for a pint or two and a game of darts—at midday, for Billy worked in the evenings, mostly. When Rosie moved, two weeks from now, they would be further apart, and Maitland would have to decide what to do. He'd find a tenant for Rosie's room, he supposed, and get his own food.

It was a bleak prospect.

He shivered.

He heard a sound.

But for the profound silence of the store, he would not have heard it; the years of walking and watching and listening had made his hearing keener. There was undoubtedly a sound. It came from near the lift. It might be a mouse, a rat, or something dislodged. He was not yet alarmed, but turned slowly toward the lift.

He heard it again: a kind of shuffling.

He stood quite still, staring. He saw nothing. He did not have his flashlight on here as there was sufficient light from the window, although not quite enough to show if anyone was there. He fumbled at his flashlight, felt his teeth clenching, turned cold and shivered. This was exactly the same as when he had seen the smash-and-grabbers.

He heard no more. Rats made a lot of noise when the store was silent. They sometimes brushed against silks and satins on display stands, or on tissue paper, on wrapping paper, even the big rollers holding the paper. At first he had wondered what had attracted them; he knew now. Assistants brought their lunch, a sandwich or two or a cake, perhaps a few biscuits or a bar of chocolate, and popped in a mouthful when no one was about. They dropped crumbs, and there were seldom any left next morning. Of course it was against the rules, but when Rosie had worked here she had often left home without any breakfast, and had needed a snack.

She'd left here the week before she married Billy. That was one good thing about Billy: he didn't want his wife to work.

"If I can't earn enough nicker to support me own wife, why get married, that's what I say."

The noise had ceased, and that worried Maitland. He himself had not made a sound or switched on his torch, had done nothing to alarm the mice or rat or rats. He knew all their tricks. They'd nibble and rustle the paper, hear him, perk up their heads, peer into the gloom and cock their little ears; and after a few seconds, if he stood still, they'd start again.

This noise was not repeated.

He was near the telephone. He could dial 999, he could sound the alarm, or he could call Archer and ask him to come down. *"If avoidable,"* ran the official Jefferson edict to night watchmen, *"never challenge intruders when alone; always call the other night watchman."*

It might not be an intruder. If he told Archer what had happened, Archer—a younger man with a sardonic outlook—would grin, and sneer. He would be sore about the dominoes, remember. This wasn't an emergency yet. Maitland kept quite still, hoping that the noise would come again, but it didn't.

He moved toward the head of the service stairs, walking very slowly and deliberately. He paused now and again but heard nothing. He stood at the head of the stairs and shone his flashlight down them. He remembered a Scotland Yard man he'd talked to on the night of the smash-and-grab, a nice chap named Peel.

"Thing to remember is that the other man's usually more scared than you are. You don't come across many of them who want to be caught."

That was certainly a thing to remember.

Was anyone here?

Maitland decided to go downstairs and have a look at the strongroom door—he needn't go far. If he saw a bright light, he would know that something was badly wrong. He went down the steps with slow deliberation, telling himself that there was nothing to be afraid of. He could not walk very quietly; the weakness in his back made absolute control of his legs difficult.

He reached the turn in the steps, heard nothing and went on.

He heard a rustling, so gentle that it might almost be imagination. He could hear something else, too—his own breathing—and an unfamiliar sound thudding inside him; it pounded slowly and remorselessly in his ears.

If it hadn't been for the tiff with Archer, he would have telephoned him.

He reached the basement floor. His light shone on the strongroom door and everything seemed all right. He tried the handle of the double doors leading to a general storeroom on the right; it should always be locked, and it was. He went across the cement floor toward the furniture storeroom, turned the handle and felt the door give. That was in order, too; the rustle of sound that he heard was not.

This was the moment of fatal error.

If Archer hadn't sneered—

Maitland pushed the door open and shone his flashlight inside. Its beam caught a mirror, hanging low, and dazzled him. He shifted it. His heart pounded, although he could hear no other sound. He saw the mirror swinging. It did not move very much, but as he shone the light into it again, the reflection moved slightly, now nearer him, now further away. No rat had touched that to make it swing. Some man had moved toward the far wall and brushed against the mirror.

Now he was quite sure.

Maitland did not turn and run, or shout, or show that he had noticed it. At first, he could do none of these things; fright paralyzed him. His teeth hurt because his jaws were clenched so tightly. Before he turned round, while he swiveled the flashlight about, he began to feel better and to think. He had often planned what he would do if he ever came across burglars again, knew it down to the last detail. He would *never* panic; that would alarm them and might lead to violence. He would behave as if he had not become suspicious, and make his way slowly toward the nearest telephone and alarm button.

He went out.

He felt sweat break out on his forehead. A shivery feeling ran up and down his spine. He wanted to run, but the training of years—army first, then civil defense, now self-discipline at Jefferson's—helped him to move slowly toward the foot of the stairs.

The pounding of the blood in his ears was so heavy that it hurt.

He gripped the handrail tightly with his left hand and the torch with his right. The man—no, the men; one man wouldn't be here by himself—would be below him. Wouldn't he? They? He needn't fear meeting any on his way. Need he?

He had to force his leaden feet to make every step. Nearing the top, nearing the spot where a man would be lying in wait if one were up there, he did not think that he would be able to go on. He felt as if someone with a hammer had got inside his chest and was pounding at him viciously. He was deaf to all sounds except those he made himself and he kept shivering, could feel sweat dripping down his forehead.

He reached the top of the staircase.

Nothing happened.

When he was sure that no one lay in wait, he became more normal. His heart still pounded, but it was steadier and not so loud. His feet no longer felt leaden, and he went more briskly toward the telephone. He had not actually seen the men downstairs, but that moving mirror was all the proof he wanted; he would just ring Archer and then dial 999.

"The police," ran the Jefferson edict, *"will reply to an urgent summons within three minutes and your duty is to endeavor to prevent the withdrawal and escape of the intruders for that period. Upon the arrival of the police you will obey their orders implicitly."*

Maitland was near the telephone. His thudding heart prevented him from hearing the faint sounds behind him. He did not look round again. He believed he had fooled the men downstairs, and if he kept his head it would be an easy capture. He actually stretched his hand out for the telephone, and, as he touched it, decided to dial 999 first and Archer afterward. His mouth was dry and his hand not very steady, but the touch of the smooth, cold instrument soothed him. Help was so near. He lifted the receiver.

He heard the crackling hum from the earpiece.

It drowned the other sound.

Then, in an awful moment of understanding, he had a terrifying preview of death, sensing the presence of the man behind him.

Before he could turn, a blow smashed onto the back of his head.

3

The Discovery

The big man, his brown coat still hanging open, fed the detonating wire to the keyhole of the safe, which was the last of five to be prepared. Flashlight batteries, standing on a small table, would start the explosions, and the five safes would be blown almost at the same time. Five consecutive thuds would come, loud inside the strongroom, but, being muffled by the papers and below street level, the noise would not travel outside. The Blower knew this job as well as a motorist knew the controls of his car, knew just how much gelignite he would need, just how tightly it should be packed, just what thickness of wall or paper was needed to muffle the sound.

He worked without haste.

The messenger, who had come back five minutes ago, and just said, "I've fixed him," was watching the Blower, hands in pocket, jimmy up his sleeve, its weight taken by his right-hand pocket. The man with the barrel-like torso was outside the door with Billy, who had not yet come round.

The messenger went out to Billy, the other man came in; both were too much on edge to keep still. The messenger pushed the door to, then lifted more stacks of paper into position, until the door was thickly lined. The Blower made no attempt to help, just watched, mouth hanging open, eyes narrowed and dull. But he did not need telling when the job was finished. He gave a little satisfied nod, walked to the flashlight batteries, and touched them with a metal bar.

The first boom came instantaneously. Then the next. The safes rocked, smoke billowed, there was a strong smell of burning explosive.

Booo-oom, went the third safe, and then the others, quickly. *Booo-oom, booo-oom.*

The air was thick when the Blower moved toward the first safe.

"Okay," he said.

They opened a door each, and began to fill the big hessian sacks with the plunder: jewelry, silver plate and a good haul of money in one-pound and ten-shilling notes, part of the day's takings. The Blower did not smile or hurry, just plunged his hand into the safe, took out as much as he could, put it into a sack, then plunged again. The others were less phlegmatic, but lost little time. They filled six sacks at four safes; the fifth contained only books and documents and these were not touched.

The moment the job was finished the Blower said:

"What's the time?"

"Two twenty-nine."

"Get a move on. We're late."

"I could screw Billy's neck, if he was okay—"

"Just get a move on, make up for it."

"Okay." Each man took a sack and hoisted it over his shoulder. Then the door was pushed open from the outside and the messenger appeared. He had pushed his cap back and the crinkly hair, growing well back on his forehead, glinted reddish in the smoky light.

"Sent him up to keep cave," he said. "The van should be there by now."

The Blower nodded.

"You never ought to have sent Billy up there; it's not his kind of job," the barrel-like man complained. "He's so jumpy, he'll—"

"Shut up," said the Blower. "You want to stay here all night?" He pushed past them, carrying his sack. The barrel-like man followed; the messenger with red hair took a third sack and went after them. They carried the sacks to the head of the stairs.

There was no sign of Maitland, who had been dragged behind a showcase.

Each man returned for another sack and, when all the loot was on the ground floor, they went through a narrow passage toward the delivery-and-parcels platform at the back of the store, then along another passage until they reached the spot where they had broken in from the bombed site.

The Blower, dragging two sacks, climbed out first.

"S'okay," Billy muttered from the darkness. There were no stars, there was no moon, street lamps were distant and dim, an airplane droned somewhere behind the heavy clouds. Not far off the sound of a car engine was audible. "They've been once, doing another circuit."

The Blower said, "Take one of these sacks and get going."

"Sure."

The others soon arrived with their booty. The car engine sounded louder, was in fact very loud when the four men and the six sacks were crowded together just below the level of the pavement in the bombed site. The car turned into this narrow street and slowed down. Before it stopped, the waiting men began to hoist the sacks up to the pavement. Two more men came from the car: one opened the trunk; the other came to carry. Even Billy dragged one to the back of the car, which was loaded within two minutes.

"Billy, you go with them. When they drop you, go straight home and don't say a word to anyone, understand?" The Blower's voice was unhurried.

"Sure, I know what I'm doing," Billy muttered. He got into the car and dropped on the seat with a sack of loot at his feet. "I'll be okay. I'm sorry—"

"Forget it." The Blower closed the door and waved the car off. It headed for Welbeck Street, then Wimpole Street, passing the surgical-instrument makers, the doctors' houses and the gleaming brass plates; at last it vanished from sight.

The Blower and the others walked to a near-by parking lot, where several cars were parked. But they didn't get into a car at once. Not far off, a light winked, and the red-haired man said, "There's a copper." They were in shadows and could see a policeman flashing his light on to shop doors, could see him trying door after door. He had not noticed them. They went into a patch of dark shadows, away from the parked cars, and stood still. The policeman drew nearer, light flashing on and off. He sauntered toward the cars, whistling faintly. The beam flashed about, going within a yard of the man with the big torso.

It missed him.

The policeman shone the light into the cars, was satisfied no one was in them, then snapped the light out, and moved off, still whistling. His footsteps were as deliberate and plodding as Jem Maitland's had been. They echoed for a long time and, when they faded, the Blower and the other man moved toward a big prewar Austin and got in. The self-starter made hardly a sound, the engine purred on a powerful note. The car moved with a kind of scornful ease, turned its back on the policeman, and moved swiftly through the deserted streets.

The Blower was at the back, the other at the front, the man with the red hair driving. He glanced down a side street, not far from the parking place, and saw a wobbling light and, vaguely against street lamps, a helmeted figure.

It was a cycling policeman.

The man with the big torso said, "Good night, Sarge." He gave a wheezy chuckle, then lit a cigarette and coughed, spluttering. The others were used to this: an attack of nerves after the event.

When he was smoking quietly, the Blower said:

"Did you truss up old Maitland?"

"No," said the driver.

"You didn't?"

"No."

"Why in hell not?"

The driver didn't answer. The Blower took out a pipe and began to fill it. The man next to the driver turned to look at him, but only saw his big, pale hands fiddling with pouch and tobacco. Soon a match scraped and flickered as the Blower lit his pipe. Strong-smelling tobacco smoke filled the car.

"That's bad," he said. "What about Billy?"

"Don't you worry about Billy," said the red-haired man. "He'll keep quiet to save his neck."

"So it's a murder rap," breathed the man with the big torso. There seemed hardly room for him to turn back and stare at the driver's profile. "You shouldn't have—"

The Blower tapped him on the shoulder.

"Shut up," he said. "Mick, go to Billy's place and stay with him. If he looks like cracking, get him away from his place for a bit, see?"

The policeman who had peered into the cars on the parking lot near Jefferson's stood in a shop doorway, drawing at a cigarette, feeling almost unpleasantly warm, for it was a muggy October night, although very clear. After a few minutes, he heard a car engine start up. It sounded surprisingly near; he knew how far sounds traveled in the quiet night, but the nearness of this one puzzled him. There were no night clubs near by; a car starting on the other side of Oxford Street wouldn't have surprised him, but this was different. Could be a doctor, from the renowned Harley and Wimpole Street blocks, but those boys were specialists; you didn't often hear of them turning out at night.

The policeman moved, holding the cigarette behind him as if the night hid prying eyes. The red light of a car was disappearing round a corner. He drew back, put the cigarette to his lips, and frowned at the reflection of the glowing tip in a window opposite. He was a man of middle age,

24

with a sergeant's stripes overdue, which meant that he was not particularly distinguished; but training often helped to stretch a thin intelligence a long way.

Night duty made a man think, too, made him fall into the habit of speaking aloud.

"Funny," he said, and forgetfully went into the street again with the cigarette at his lips. Now there was no sound of any kind anywhere. "Might have been from that parking lot at Middle's." He pushed his helmet back, scratched, and then moved back toward the parking lot. He had finished his rounds ten minutes or so early to make time for the cigarette, and the sergeant wasn't due for a while. He would soon turn into this street on his bicycle.

The policeman, named Egerton, walked back to the cars, cupping his cigarette in his right hand when he wasn't drawing at it. If he knew the Sarge, the Sarge was doing the same. He reached the parking lot and looked at the cars. There were four.

There had been five.

You did not have to be a brilliant officer to notice that kind of thing, especially as it was illegal to park here all night, according to the strict letter of the law.

The policeman drew at the cigarette, glanced along the road and saw the sergeant's wavering bicycle lamp. He dropped the cigarette and trod it out, and was waiting at the corner when the sergeant, named Madd, came up, bicycle wheels whirring. Madd was one of the tall, bullet-headed type, younger than Egerton and sometimes aggressive.

"Hallo, Egg. All okay?" Doubt tinged the sergeant's voice.

"I think so, Sarge," Egerton said. "But a car started off just now; it—"

"I saw it."

"Did you? Big old Austin, prewar."

"All I can say," said the sergeant, "is that it had a nicely tuned engine. Didn't hear a sound until I saw it; gave me quite a turn. This is it, Egg, we report this parking all night. Better put it down while the details are fresh in your mind. And take the numbers. See another car?"

"No."

"It's a funny thing," Sergeant Madd said, "but I was down by Lewis's when a big Yankee car passed, an old Packard. I had a word with Fiddler and it turned up again—driver might have lost his way, I suppose."

"I suppose," agreed Egerton. He started a round of the cars, taking the numbers, trying to recall that of the old Austin. He remembered that it began with B, but couldn't get any further. He did not try this because he thought there was any significance attached to the Austin, but as a test of memory—he had only glanced at the number plate once, and the light wasn't good.

He finished scribbling in his little black notebook.

"Okay, Sarge."

"Let's go and see Fiddler," the sergeant said, and, wheeling his bicycle, he walked with P.C. Egerton toward Oxford Street. The end building was the massive edifice of Jefferson's Store, famous throughout London, England, and most of the world. It was several stories higher than any near-by building, and the lighted windows shone brightly; that particular corner was almost as light as day.

"Lumme, I'm hungry tonight!" Egerton exclaimed. "Funny how it takes you, ain't it? Some nights—"

He stopped short, jerked his head up, and felt as if an electric shock had passed through his body. Sergeant Madd started so violently that he almost lost control of the bicycle, but grabbed it.

An alarm bell clattered into the silence, so loud that it deafened them. After the first moment of astonishment they began to move, Sergeant Madd flinging a leg across his bicycle and pedaling furiously toward the corner before Egerton got into his stride. There was no need to blow a whistle; every man on duty for a mile around would hear that raucous alarm bell—it was Jefferson's, with its unmistakable clangor.

A figure appeared against the doorway of the store as Sergeant Madd drew up. He jumped off his bicycle, let it fall, and ran toward the doorway, drawing out his truncheon as he moved. But this was a night watchman, a big, tall, long-jawed man, his mouth wide open in fright as he unlocked the door and pulled back the bolts. He jerked the door open as Sergeant Madd reached him. The lights from the windows heightened his pallor; he looked sick, terrified.

"Bur-burglars," he stammered. "C-can't see them, b-but old Maitland's dead, h-h-head smashed in. I—I didn't know, I—didn't know, I—d-didn't know, I was upstairs, I—"

"Take it easy," Madd said sharply. "Easy, now." He gripped the other's shoulder with powerful, hurtful fingers. Egerton came hurrying. "Get to a telephone, Egg, call the Yard—you dialed 999?" Madd asked the night watchman.

"N-n-no, I—"

"Get cracking, Egg," said Sergeant Madd. "Let's see this chap you say's been murdered," he added to the night watchman, and they hurried into the shop. "How many of you here?"

"Two. J-j-just two. Jem Maitland and me, God it's awful, and I was upstairs, I—"

"Take it easy." Madd gripped his arm more tightly and then stopped short. A light was on over some showcases near the lift, shining down from the ceiling onto Jem Maitland, and onto Jem Maitland's head. Blood-matted hair, little rivulets and a pool of blood, the crumpled body, the slack mouth and half-closed eyes told their own story. "Poor devil," Madd said. He was sure that the old man was dead, but knelt down quickly and felt his pulse. He stayed like that, with the limp hand in his, while the other night watchman looked on dumbly and Egerton spoke to the Information Room at Scotland Yard.

4

Roger West

Roger West, lying on his left side and looking into
his wife's face, felt a drowsy, sensuous content-
ment. He had been awake for five minutes, but
nothing made him want to get up. The light was
poor. Rain spattered the big window. Wind was
forcing down the top branches of the two plane
trees he could see, and leaves were flying from the
twigs, some dropping straight down, others whisk-
ing upward; a few pattered against the window.

He was warm and snug, and felt good.

It was good to lie by the side of one's wife, feel
the warmth of her body against one, look into her
face and be able to smile, to study the dark lashes
curling against cheeks still tanned from a late holi-
day in October's Indian summer. It was good to
want to kiss the full, warm lips, to be surprised
again by the three tiny moles grouped close to one
corner of her mouth and to be amused by the little
puffing sound she made as she breathed. She was
in a deep sleep; she always slept heavily in the
morning.

29

Her hair, in a heavy sleeping net because she had had a permanent only a few days ago, had escaped at one side, and that wouldn't please her. There were strands of gray—almost streaks of gray—in that dark hair. He remembered her talking about having a color rinse, whatever that might mean, and saying that she'd decided not to, it was better to grow old gracefully.

He heard a creaking sound of a door opening and immediately became more wakeful. Soon, whispered voices told him that both their sons, Martin called Scoopy and Richard called Richard, were up and in the playroom. From that moment on, Roger couldn't rest. He pushed the bedclothes back and got out of bed carefully. A striking clock chimed with unexpected clarity—five, six, seven. A squall of rain sent leaves cracking against the window. Filthy morning. He took a dressing gown off the back of a chair and picked up cigarettes and a lighter from the chair seat, thrust his feet into slippers and went out.

A light was on in the playroom—really the spare room, which now served a double purpose. Shadows moved and a whirring sound broke the quiet with a stealthy note. Roger stepped to the door without being heard and looked in.

Martin, the ten-year-old, was squatting massively by the side of the electric train set screwed to the floor, and, with great earnestness, watching the locomotive, the tender and three carriages moving slowly round. Richard, just nine, stood by the window, barefooted and with his dressing gown wide open. Alternately he looked into the leaf-strewn, wind-racked garden and at the moving train.

Neither of the boys noticed Roger.

"Make it go faster," Richard said, rubbing one of his large ears, which jutted from his long, pleasing face. He had a pink-and-white complexion, without blemish: a girl's dream.

"If you make it go any faster with this load on, it might blow a fuse," said Martin realistically. "Dad said if we blew any more fuses we'd jolly well have to pay for new ones out of our own pocket money, and it's always you, you oaf, overloading it."

"Oo, it isn't. And what's the use of having an electric train set if you can't pull goods along with it, that's what I want to know." Richard, swiftly aggressive in self-defense, moved from the window, his big blue eyes flashing. "Anyway, I don't *want* it to crawl like that, and I'll pay for the old fuses if they blow. *I'm* not mean." Darting downward, his hand moved toward the control switch.

Swift as the movement was, Martin's large hand got there first.

"Oh, no, you don't! I happen to know you haven't got any money, so that means I'd have to pay, as usual."

"Oo, you wouldn't! Anyway, I'd pay you back. And I don't s'pose Dad meant—"

The telephone bell rang, sharp and startling. Both boys looked up and saw their father, but were too startled by the ringing to speak. Roger grinned, shook a fist at Richard and hurried back to the bedroom. Janet was stirring, for the bell was making a hell of a din. This was the Yard, of course; the most likely time for emergency calls was between five o'clock and seven. If anything happened on one of his jobs later than seven, the

31

night men usually waited until he reached the office.

"Roger West here."

"Morning, Mr. West, this is Sergeant Keen. Sorry to disturb you, but a job's come in that the Night Super thinks you ought to know about. The Gelignite Gang again, and very ugly. A night watchman was murdered."

"Where?" Roger put the question automatically.

"Jefferson's, Oxford Street. Not much doubt the G.G. was behind it. There are all the usual signs down in the strongroom, blown safes and stacks of paper—they might as well use a trade-mark. The Super says can you go straight there?"

"What's his hurry to get me on the job?"

"There's another night watchman, sir—chap named Archer. He's nearly all in, but the Super thinks you ought to have a word with him before he's given a sedative and has some shut-eye. You'll almost certainly get a G.G. job. Nothing like getting at them before they've had time to forget, and—"

"Hold this chap Archer for half an hour or so, will you? I won't be any longer."

"Right, sir."

"Anything there to help us?"

"Well—there is and there isn't. There was a pretty good Divisional sergeant on duty last night, chap named Madd—two d's, sir—and he and a copper saw a car moving off from a parking lot near Jefferson's. The Super thinks you ought to see them before they go off duty, too."

"I will, thanks. Did the murdered chap suffer much?"

"Shouldn't think so," the Yard man said. "They cracked his skull like an eggshell."

Roger said, "All right, thanks. Good-by," and rang off.

Janet was wide awake and looking at him from her clear eyes, gray-green and very bright. Richard was kneeling on the foot of the big double bed, still barefooted, those enormous eyes as blue as summer sky and rounded and eager.

"Oo, Dad, was it *murder?*"

Roger was startled into silence.

"*Was it?*" breathed Richard.

"One of these days you're going to have to learn that ninety-nine crimes out of a hundred are not crimes of violence," Roger said very slowly, and added with mock severity: "And if you blow that fuse by overloading the set, I'll halve your pocket money for a couple of weeks."

"Oh, you wouldn't!"

"Wouldn't I?"

"Course not! Dad, was it?"

"What?"

"Murder?"

"Why *must* all boys be so bloodthirsty?" Janet demanded, hitching herself up in bed and then grabbing the sheets and drawing them up to her bare shoulders in obvious alarm; she hadn't a stitch on. Roger grinned. "Richard, where are your slippers?" Janet demanded sharply.

"In my room, I forgot. Sorry. I say, Dad, *is it?*"

"Go and put them on at once."

"Oh, Mum—"

Roger said quietly, "Yes, Fish, a man was murdered. Murder is a very nasty business, you know, and nothing for us to be excited about. This man

33

might have children, like you, and a wife. Think how unhappy they'd all be about it."

Richard's eyes misted over slightly. He nodded very slowly and got off the bed. As slowly, he went out of the room, the belt of his dressing gown dragging behind him. As soon as the pink heels had disappeared, Janet dropped the sheet and said:

"Quick, give me my nightdress before they come in again." She looked round and couldn't see it. "Where on earth—"

Roger grinned, grabbed the sheet and blanket and raised them a foot above her. She gave a muffled *"Don't!"* and snatched the pale green nightdress, a flimsy heap close to her side.

"A fat lot of difference that makes," Roger scoffed. He leaned over the bed and looked into her eyes, then kissed her. "Good morning, darling. I've been called out, but blessed are the understanding sergeants who don't wake me too early in the morning. If I can, I'll get back for breakfast."

"You won't be within a mile for breakfast," Janet said scornfully. She was sitting up in bed and struggling into her nightdress. Roger stood watching for a few moments, feeling a gathering tightness in his chest, remembering last night and this morning's drowsy snugness. He forgot the murdered night watchman, the Gelignite Gang, everything but Janet. Then, outside, cups and saucers clinked on a tray; Janet tucked the nightdress down and Roger said:

"That's old Scoop with the tea. I'd better get some clothes on." His clothes were folded over a chair, and he began to slide into them.

Martin called Scoopy came in, already five feet

34

three inches tall, lean but very broad, with a large, open face, a good skin with one or two tiny patches of spots just beneath the surface. His gray eyes had a mature gravity, but his hair was like a mop. He put the tea tray down on the bedside table.

"Morning, Mum, morning, Dad! Thought you'd have to go rushing off, so I made the tea early."

"Bless you!" Janet stretched out her hands. "Come and—"

"What's the matter with Richard?" asked Martin, submitting soberly to a good-morning kiss.

"Nothing, is there?" Janet looked startled.

Roger, slipping into a pair of underpants, shrugged his shoulders resignedly. He was nearly six feet tall, his arms and shoulders looked powerful, his hips were narrow, his lean legs well muscled and his stomach as flat as a board. At forty, few men could be fitter.

"Richard!" Janet called.

"He's crying," announced Scoopy.

"But I wasn't really cross, I just told him to go and put his slippers on. Roger—" Janet shot a reproachful look at Roger, who was now sliding his arms through the armholes of a singlet—"you shouldn't have threatened to halve his pocket money, you know he's desperately anxious to get that bike, and—"

From the door, Richard said huskily, "It wasn't that."

He came in slowly, feet dragging in the felt slippers. His belt still hung down. His eyes were moist and tears had rolled down his cheeks; he was sniffing and groping in his pockets as if for a handkerchief. He went straight to Janet, who put an arm round him with reassuring welcome. He clung to

35

her. Martin contemplated all this for a moment, then shrugged and turned to his father with an old-fashioned, "Oh, what's the matter with the baby now?" look.

"Pour the tea, Scoop," Roger said, picking up his shirt.

"Yes, all right."

"Richard, what's upset you like this?" Janet made the child look at her; he still clung tightly, as if fearful. "Darling, Daddy didn't mean it, and I—"

Richard said in a quavering voice, "It's—it's that poor man. And perhaps—perhaps he has a wife, like you, and some children. And I—I didn't *care*, I was just excited. I *hate* myself. I really do."

Janet stared speechlessly at him and at Roger. Scoopy poured out the tea with great deliberation, then broke the silence—and shook both his parents badly. He spoke as if he had given this problem deep thought, but was still puzzled.

"Daddy, what makes men do wicked things like murder and robbery and—well, all those criminal things? Do you remember that man we met in the street the other day, who spoke to you ever so nicely? He seemed a jolly decent type, and looked kind, I thought, and yet he'd been in prison for five years for stealing, hadn't he? That's what Sergeant Morgan's son told me, anyway. I wish I understood. Could you tell me?"

Richard, hearing all this, became intrigued. The storm of remorse faded as, hopefully, he watched Roger. They all watched Roger as he looped a tie round his neck, knotted it, turned down his collar, then picked up a cup of tea and sipped.

The boys' interest began to flag. Richard turned to his mother, obviously not expecting an answer, no longer so taut with emotion; he would be all right now.

Martin looked disappointed but resigned.

Then Roger said quietly, "I haven't time to go into it now, Scoop, but with nine out of ten of these chaps, it's due to a bad beginning in life. Perhaps they're not taught the difference between right and wrong. Their parents may not care a jot how they get their money. Or they might be orphans. They might live in the slums, and possibly have no money to buy food with. So they drift into crime. Once you've started, it's hard to stop. At first it seems easy, and no one finds out, so you steal or cheat again, and then—well, the law always catches up. But—" He sipped the tea again, groped for his cigarettes, then went on slowly and deliberately. "But some people seem to be born bad. I can't explain that."

There was a long pause in which Richard nodded solemnly but didn't speak.

"I think I understand." Martin's gaze was very direct; his broad, open face tugged at Roger's emotions. "How do you know if a man's born bad, though? I mean, could I be? Or Richard? Or—"

"It would have shown long ago if you were," Roger interrupted briskly. His voice was louder. "I give you my word I haven't seen any sign of it in either of you." He grinned and tweaked Martin's ear. "Except old Fish, who wants to blow the train-set fuses and then make you and me pay for them! I'll tan his hide if he gets up to those tricks again."

Richard, startled at the "except old Fish," was soon grinning broadly. He pulled himself free from Janet, scampered round the bed and leaped at

Roger, who grunted as four stone eight pounds of wiry boy thudded into him.

"Careful, old chap!"

"Daddy, could Scoopy and me, I mean I, could we come with you to the Yard?" Richard burst out. "We could come back by bus, there's plenty of time, Mum could be cooking the breakfast. Oh, please say 'yes,' we haven't had a ride for days."

"If you're both ready in five minutes, yes," said Roger. "I can't wait a second longer."

Martin's expression changed to one of delight, and the boys darted toward the door, racing to get into their room first. Richard suddenly burst into laughter.

Janet, leaning back on the pillows, took a cup of tea from Roger. Roger finished his and said:

"Save us from the ones that are born bad. I'll have a man put them on the bus."

"They'll be all right," Janet said.

5

Rosie Mulcaster

Rosie Mulcaster, the dead night watchman's daughter, woke about the same time as the telephone bell rang at the Wests' home. She did not stir for some minutes. It was gloomy at the window, and she could hear gusts of wind sending the rain spattering over the glass. Across the road, a light was on in a tiny front room—one as tiny as this. All the houses in Brickett Street were identical in size and shape, and most were in the same state of disrepair. Once newly painted house, a few doors away, looked stark and out of place.

Billy was snoring.

Rosie thought, "I'm not going to like getting up, but I must." She didn't stir, for she was comfortable lying on her back, although aware of the strangeness of carrying the child. A few days ago the doctor had confirmed her guess, her dream; she was three months gone. On getting up in the mornings, and just occasionally during the day—especially when she smelled frying oil—she felt the nausea; so far that was the only discomfort.

It must be nearly seven.

Her father would be home by half past, for the night watchmen at Jefferson's were relieved at seven sharp, and Dad caught the same bus with unvarying punctuality; it had a quick run through the empty streets. He would be wet and tired—he often looked very tired lately—and his back would hurt. She wished she weren't going to leave him, but Billy was emphatic; he couldn't stand it here any longer, they had to have their own place.

Rosie turned over on her side and eased herself up. Then she pushed the bedclothes back and sat on the side of the bed, almost fearfully. She wore a flimsy nightdress which clung to her rounding figure. The first thing that had attracted Billy, that attracted all the boys, was her figure. There wasn't anything she could do about it, and after all, the curves were in the right places. She didn't flaunt them like some girls, either; the fact that she was thickening at the waist didn't worry her at all.

Billy didn't move.

She felt the nausea, which was now almost a part of her life, as she stood there. After a moment or two, she felt better, and her hopes rose. Perhaps she was nearly over the sickness; the doctor had said that it seldom lasted much longer than the third or fourth month. She certainly felt better more quickly than she had yesterday. She slid her small, white feet into heelless slippers, and put on a lovely silk dressing gown with a pattern of red tulips: a present from Billy. She turned to look at her husband. His face was near the window, and the light showed a swelling just on the side of his jaw; it was reddish, too, and quite a lump.

"What on earth is that?" she began.

Billy stirred.

She didn't want to wake him; he was liable to become bad-tempered if she woke him when getting up to make tea and get "supper" for her father. She frowned at the bruise, wondered how he'd got it, then went out, closing the door very quietly. Then she listened, to make sure that Billy didn't turn over in bed or get up.

Rosie heard nothing.

There were two rooms and a toilet up here, one room and a kitchen and scullery downstairs; many smaller hovels survived in London, but it was still a hovel. The woodwork was freshly painted, and one of the walls had been distempered only that spring; it still gave off a slightly acrid smell. The linoleum on the stairs had lost all newness, though. She went down cautiously, because if she hurried the stairs would creak.

Billy was at his worst in the mornings, but she couldn't really grumble; there was nothing else the matter with him. He worked at a restaurant in the West End and was seldom home before three, sometimes much later. She had waked up when he had come in last night, but he had only grunted when she had spoken, and she had been so drowsy.

She reached the foot of the stairs and the narrow passage leading to the front door.

Usually she turned left, stepping straight into the kitchen. That had just a deal-topped table and four Windsor chairs, as well as a stained deal dresser. But it was clean, and they had all their meals there. She actually stepped inside, finding just enough daylight coming through the small window to show the gas stove, the matches on it, and the aluminum kettle, when she heard a sound in the front room.

It was like a grunt.

She turned round quickly.

The sound came again—more snore than grunt. It set her heart beating fast, but after a moment she told herself that it was Dad, who had come home early, or else it was later than she thought.

But he wouldn't drop asleep; he would want some tea and something to eat.

She moved across the kitchen, forgetting how much better she felt, snatched the matches off the gas stove, turned back, reached the front-room door, and struck a match. As the match flared, the snoring stopped abruptly. A man was lying on the old horsehair sofa. He was fully dressed except for his shoes and a collar and tie, and struggling to get up. He was reaching under the sofa, too. The light wasn't very bright, but it glinted on his red hair. Something in his manner frightened her; he seemed to be in a panicky kind of hurry. His eyes looked small, his mouth was thin and set tightly.

Rosie gasped, *"Who are you?"*

He stopped fighting to sit up, and relaxed. He licked his lips and worked his mouth as if he were parched. Snorers often were. He had very little hair in front but a bushy mop at the back, curly and wiry and the color of dull copper. His nose was flattened and his face was an odd shape, wide at the forehead and between the ears, narrowing sharply until it tapered to nothing at his pointed chin. He sat up and grinned, then scratched his head.

"Looking for someone, ducky!"

"What—what are you doing here?"

"Just having a nap," said the red-haired man. "Billy Mulcaster invited me to share his humble abode wiv' him anytime I needed it." That was more sneer than laugh. "How is Billy?" He paused, ears cocked, and the noise of Billy's snoring came faintly through the ceiling. "He sounds okay, Rosie love. You are Rosie, aren't you?"

"I—yes. Yes, but he didn't—he didn't tell me."

"Wouldn't want to wake his sweetie up, would he?" asked the red-haired man.

The light seemed better now that Rosie was used to it, and she could see everything about the man; she disliked it, too. But the thing which she noticed most vividly was the piece of iron on the floor by the sofa. She knew, now that she was less nervous, that this man had been in a panic to push it under the sofa, to stop her from seeing it. Or had he been trying to get it? It was about a foot long, and she knew the name for it: a burglar's jimmy. She wished she hadn't seen it, wished that the man wasn't here, a "friend" of Billy.

"What got you up so early?" the man asked.

"I—I'm gong to make some tea," she said, uneasily. "My—my father will be here soon."

"Will he?"

"Yes, he—he works at night. I—I must put the kettle on." Rosie went out, disliking the way the man looked at her. Something in his expression when she had talked about her father working at nights had scared her again, but she told herself that it was just fancy. Billy shouldn't have invited him here; perhaps he'd had a few drinks too many.

She lit the pilot of the gas lamp in the kitchen, then pulled the little chain; white light glowed from the mantle, a soft hissing sound came. Next she lit the ring under the kettle, and saw, from the tinny-looking, round-faced alarm clock on the mantelpiece above the fireplace, that it was twenty-five minutes to eight. Dad would be here any minute. She began to lay the table: knives, forks, bread, butter, and marmalade, putting all of these on one end of the table, which was covered with a plastic cloth in big red-and-blue squares. Then she fetched the bacon from a tiny larder.

She didn't like that man at all. Where had Billy got that bruise from? Why was Dad late?

She did not consciously connect the three thoughts; they were just on her mind. By five to eight, she was beginning to worry; her father had never been so late. She hadn't yet made the tea, but was thirsty and beginning to feel a touch of nausea again.

She heard a movement in the doorway.

The red-haired man, still in his socks, grinned at her.

"Got a cuppa for an old pal?"

"I'm just going to make it," she said. "You can have a cup when it's ready." She wished he would go away, but he didn't. He came further into the kitchen, sat on a corner of the table, and just looked at her. She knew that kind of look only too well. Some men could give it so easily, could make a girl's face go turkey red just by staring her up and down; other men didn't know how. Billy didn't; but this man—

She made the tea.

When she put the brown teapot on a tray the stranger was still looking at her, but at her face now; he was smiling as if at a joke. She pushed a cup of tea across to him and he said, "Ta." He had

44

big hands, and his broad nails were bitten down, making the tops of the fingers thick and repulsive. He started to pick at a brown stain on his coat. She noticed that, and was startled when he snatched his hand away and thrust it into his pocket. He had gone white. He glared at her intently, then picked up the teacup in his left hand and sipped. After a few seconds, he laughed.

"You can make good char," he said. "Don't Billy have one?"

"Not—not until he calls."

"Lucky old man," said the red-haired stranger. "And I don't mean maybe!" That roving, calculating look came again, and his lips were curved in the smile she didn't like. "You shouldn't spoil him."

"I can't understand about Dad," Rosie said. The clock said five past eight. "I haven't known him as late as this for years."

"He'll get here," said the red-haired man, and sipped his tea again. "Don't he always?"

At a quarter to nine, Rosie was nearly in a panic. Billy was still upstairs, asleep; whenever she paused to listen she could hear his snoring. The stranger had been up to see him twice, and come down without making a sound; each time, she had been startled to find him so near. Now he was washing at the scullery sink, spluttering and splashing, and she stood at the front door, looking toward the corner nearest the Whitechapel Road and the bus stop. It was raining hard, and blustering; newspapers, bus tickets, cigarette cartons, litter of all kinds swept along the narrow street or eddied in a miniature whirlwind. People walked to and fro, but her father didn't show up.

She felt a hand on her arm.

"Oh!" she gasped, and swung round. It was the red-haired stranger, standing just behind her. He didn't take his hand away. "You scared me. I wish you wouldn't creep about like that!"

"Only want to be a pal," he said. "Like me to go and phone Jefferson's?" She had told him where her father worked, talked freely and agitatedly although she disliked him.

"Oh, yes, please!"

"Okay." He unhooked a raincoat from the back of the front door and shrugged himself into it. There was a dark patch on his coat, and vaguely Rosie realized that it was where the brown spot had been; he'd washed it off.

She wished he would hurry.

He winked at her and went out without looking back. He was slightly bandy-legged and pigeon-toed, and she still disliked him intensely, but not many men would have gone out into the rain to do this for her; you never could tell. She watched until he turned the corner, than went back and closed the door. She ought to get dressed, even if that meant waking Billy; it was late enough, anyhow.

Billy didn't wake.

The red-haired man didn't come back as quickly as she expected him. By half-past nine, she had been to the front door several times to look for him; the last time, she saw two policemen standing at the corner. That often happened; the police had a lot of customers in and near Brickett Street. Rosie didn't give them a second thought, except

46

about the possibility of telling them that her father wasn't home yet, and asking if there'd been an accident. But the red-haired man would soon be back with news, wouldn't he?

Rosie went to the door again.

'A car had stopped by the side of the two policemen, and a man got out of it. He was tall and moved very briskly, with a kind of springy step which was very noticeable. In the murky morning light she saw that he was good-looking, and wore a beige-colored raincoat, with a brown trilby pushed to the back of his head showing his fair hair.

Rosie did not want to be seen staring at the police; it might make them think that she was nervous of them. She was not, had never been, and knew that her father had never broken the law in any way that counted. All the same, the police were people to avoid; they were the enemies of many who lived in the neighborhood, and the friends of none.

It was as if they came from a different, hostile world.

She busied herself in the kitchen, but couldn't keep her mind off her father or the long absence of the red-haired man. If he didn't come back soon, she would have to go out and telephone; it wouldn't hurt her, and if Billy woke—

There was a sharp knock at the front door.

She rushed to open it, expecting Billy's friend, not her father, for her father had a key.

Instead, the man who had been talking to the policemen stood there. He was so good-looking, in a nice way, that he took her mind off her worries for a moment; the way one noticed a striking hat, even after a quarrel. It was his brief silence and the gravity of his expression which combined to frighten her. She felt her heart hammering, and clutched at the door, almost afraid that she would fall.

He said gravely, "Are you Mrs. Mulcaster—Mr. Maitland's daughter?"

She said, "Yes, that's right, I'm—I'm Rosie Mai —Rosie Mulcaster. Who—"

"I'm an officer from Scotland Yard," the caller told her. "My name is West." Unexpectedly, he held out his hand; he held hers tightly and for a split second longer than necessary. Was he a fresh type? He didn't look it, as he scanned her face without dropping his gaze; he seemed to be searching for something in her eyes.

Nausea came sneaking up on her, and she turned dizzy. The caller took her arm and helped her into the front room; his guiding hand was very firm.

"I'm afraid I've some bad news for you, Mrs. Mulcaster." The voice had a steadying quality and did a little to offset the fear his words created. "Sit down, and—"

"No, I—I'm all right. I'd rather stand. Is it—is it Dad? He's—he's over two hours late."

The man who called himself West of Scotland Yard answered in that quiet voice, "I'm very, very sorry. Yes, it is about your father." He paused, and his hand touched her arm. She was too horrified to see the strain at his eyes, or suspect how much he disliked this task. "He met with a serious accident, and I'm afraid—"

She did not hear the rest, but swayed, felt black mists filling her head, felt her knees bend. Then suddenly a kind of strength poured into her. She wanted to deny all this; it wasn't true, it couldn't

48

be true about her Dad. *It couldn't* be true. Then all her pent-up dread burst out.

"*No, no, no!*" she cried. She shook clenched fists. "It can't be true, not my Dad. *No!*"

"I only wish—" began West.

"It can't be true!" she screamed, and almost choked as she caught her breath.

Before West could speak again, there was a thump above their heads, and a man called clearly, "What the hell!"

6

Billy

West saw the girl's horrified face, the pallor, the burning brightness of her eyes. There was something here he didn't understand, a long-lying strain born out of a tension which was due to some factor much greater than her father's lateness. Her voice was shrill and piercing, her small hands were tightly clenched, and the solitaire diamond of her engagement ring glittered with spurious brightness. It was so big that it hardly seemed real—rhinestone, paste, or glass? She was a little Juno of a woman, not much higher than his shoulder but magnificently built. Her hair was dishevelled, and there were metal curlers at the back and sides.

"Rosie!" bellowed the man upstairs. "Rosie!"

"It can't be true, not my Dad," cried Rosie. Her strength slipped away from her, she lurched forward and gripped West's hands for support. "Please, please, he's not dead, he can't be."

West didn't speak.

"Oh, Dad, Dad!" she sobbed. "Oh, Dad!"

Footsteps clattered on the narrow staircase; it sounded as if the wall were going to crash down. Rosie's head fell heavily against his shoulder, and her words became incoherent; she was just sobbing.

Over her head, West saw Billy Mulcaster.

Afterward, he remembered that first meeting with unexpected vividness. It wasn't quite real, and that was not wholly due to the emotional storm which racked the girl. It was Billy Mulcaster's entrance, like that of a man in a strange melodrama appearing suddenly in a doorway, one hand clenched and raised, the other holding the door frame tightly. He was tall and quite startlingly handsome. His dark hair, some hanging over his forehead, was sleek and overlong, his dark stubble was like a blue shadow on his cheeks and jaw, and there was a red bruise on one side. His dark eyes were bleary. He wore pale blue pajamas, the jacket unbuttoned, the trousers slipping down. He was too thin, and he looked alarmed—frightened?—but no, he wasn't quite real. This was like a pose, but Mulcaster's handsomeness wasn't; that was real, triumphing over all the odds against it.

Rosie was huddled against West, sobbing, shivering.

"What the hell are *you* doing?" Billy demanded, but he didn't move away from the doorway. His voice had a slight twang, but it wasn't true Cockney. He hitched up his trousers and licked his lips.

"I've brought your wife some bad news," West said.

"What the hell do you mean?" Billy still didn't move, but he lowered his head and appeared to watch Roger warily. "What kind of bad news?"

"Her father is dead." West paused, then added the word he hadn't meant to use in front of Rosie Mulcaster just yet. "Murdered."

Billy's hand slid off the door frame. He raised both hands, lightly clenched, to his chest. He licked his lips again, and his gaze shifted away from Roger toward the window, to the fireplace, then to his wife's back.

"Gawd, no," he breathed.

"I'm afraid it's true," Roger West said. There were a lot of things about this interview which ran oddly, but he had little chance to think of them, for Rosie moved away from him suddenly, turning toward Billy and stretching out her hands.

Billy mouthed, "No." He didn't move toward her at first, but she called his name and suddenly he was jolted into action. He rushed forward. "Oh, sweetie, this is hell! Just hell." He crushed her in his arms, and buried his face in her hair. And she kept sobbing. He didn't look up, seemed to forget that anyone else was there.

Someone knocked at the front door.

Billy looked up. "What—" he began, and gulped. "Would you mind?"

West said, "Of course not," and turned and opened the door.

The man who stood there was a stranger whose appearance he didn't like at all: a short man with a trilby pushed to the back of his head, coppered-colored hair growing well back and thin at the temples. Greenish eyes narrowed in an odd-shaped face holding an oddly insolent expression. He had both hands in the pockets of a raincoat which looked soaked through.

"Who're you?" he demanded.

West said, "I'm from the police." He didn't move to one side—and although he saw the glance which the caller darted toward Billy, he turned too late to see the new horror on Billy's face; all he saw was the top of Billy's head as the youth buried his face in his wife's hair. "I've brought Mrs. Mulcaster some bad news."

"That's a shame," the red-haired man said. "How bad?"

"Her father was murdered last night."

"That *so*," breathed the red-haired man. "Gee, that *is* bad. Murdered? Poor old guy." He moved forward, and Roger stood aside. "This is the time a guy wants a pal." He pushed past West. "Anything I can do, Billy? I'd just been and telephoned Jefferson's for Rosie, but they were cagey, didn't let on. Poor old guy."

"It's awful, isn't it?" Billy said thickly. He glanced at West, then quickly back at the red-haired man. Rosie wasn't crying now. West saw that she was holding her body stiffly. At her best, she was really something to look at, he imagined— her profile was startlingly good, and her figure would shame Jane Russell. "Rosie, I don't know what to say, I just don't know what to say," Billy muttered.

Her eyes were red-rimmed and puffy. She looked desperately ill as Billy helped her across to the sofa.

"Whyn't you make her a cuppa char?" asked the red-haired man. "Or give her a nip o' brandy. Awful shock, this musta' been." He stood in the middle of the little room as if he owned the place, then shot a question at West. "You from Mort Place?"

Mort Place held the headquarters of the Division which controlled this part of London.

"No, the Yard."

"Well, fancy a Yard dick taking the trouble to come and tell the girl in person," marveled the red-haired man. "Must be getting soft-hearted." He grinned. "Thanks, Guv'nor, but Billy and me will look after her now." He glanced over his shoulder. "Won't we, Billy?"

Billy was halfway into the kitchen.

"Sure," he said. "Sure."

"So thanks a million," the red-haired man said.

West, poker-faced until then, gave a swift, startling smile. It thrust vitality into his good looks, made his face alert and arresting. He moved, too, with quick, brisk movements, took out a cigarette case and a box of matches, and offered the case.

The redhead took a cigarette.

"Ta."

They lit up.

"Ta."

"I'm very glad that her husband's at home to look after her," West said, briskly. "And you—are you a relative?"

"Eh? Oh, no, just a pal. We're working at the same place just now, Billy and me." The man didn't volunteer his name.

"I see. Lucky you were here, for Mr. Mulcaster looks as if he'll take it badly, too." There were sounds of running water, and the gas popped when Billy lit it. "I'm sure you know how it is," West went on. "Mr. Maitland was a night watchman at Jefferson's, and was fatally injured—they couldn't save him." He watched the redhead closely, but the narrowed green eyes were expressionless. "It was a well-planned burglary; the murderers got in while he was on one of the upper floors, and lay in wait for him. That makes it look as if they knew what his movements were likely to be, and timed the raid accordingly." West was still smiling, still very brisk—and he had attracted Rosie's attention. She was sitting upright and staring at him. Billy had come back to the doorway, also to stare. "If we act quickly we might get the murderers at once," West went on. He glanced at Rosie, sensing her quickening interest. "I don't want to make thing worse for Mrs. Mulcaster, but it's possible that someone has been pumping her father lately—someone who struck up an acquaintance, perhaps, and found out what time he would be upstairs, leaving the basement and ground floor empty."

West stopped, invitingly.

The red-haired man didn't speak.

Rosie said in shaky voice, "Dad wouldn't talk to anyone about his job. Dad was—Dad was quite trustworthy, see? He knew his duty, and—"

Tears welled up, and she dropped back, bowing her head, her shoulders quaking again.

"Look, Guv'nor, why don't you skip?" asked the redhead, putting a big hand on West's arm. The fingers were thick, red and ugly. West glanced down at them and disliked the thought of the hand touching his: an odd, irrational prejudice. "I'll tell you what, if Billy and me can find out about anyone who pumped old Maitland, okay, I'll let you know. What's your handle?"

West freed his arm, took out his wallet, and put a card into the man's hand.

"All right, telephone me. It might be important.

I'd better have your name so that I can make sure you're put through to me."

The red-haired man was staring at the card. His lips set very tightly, his mouth had gone very small. Suddenly the tip of his tongue shot out.

"So you're Mr. West! Strewth, never expected to meet a top man of the Yard face to face, Mr. West." He gave a quick, leery grin. "If I can do you a favor, I certainly will. Name of O'Leary. Mike O'Leary, 27 Nattur Street, will find me any time." He put out his hand.

West shook it, and felt the surge of irrational prejudice again. He turned to Rosie, who was now sitting back and staring straight in front of her. Billy was coming in with two cups of tea. It all looked normal, natural, homely, pathetic. There was Rosie with all the promise of her beauty marred by taut nerves; Billy with his film-star handsomeness; O'Leary—

O'Leary ushered West to the door.

"I'll say good-by to them for you. Very sad, this is; they've only been married six months, and Rosie's in the family way. Loved her old Dad, she did, and you know what women are when they're like *this*. But don't you worry, Mr. West, I'll find a way of questioning her, and if there's anything I can tell you, I'll telephone the Yard. Might even call in person, if it's important. That be okay?"

"Telephone me first, will you?"

"Oh, sure, sure."

West stepped onto the pavement, and the door closed on his heels. He had a feeling that he had been pushed out, smoothly, firmly. That didn't worry him. At the end of the street two policemen were standing by his car, a new black Wolseley, sleek and fast and with a specially tuned engine.

The thing to remember was that in Brickett Street, in fact in the whole neighborhood, including Nattur Street, there was a silent, sometimes subconscious antagonism toward the police. It made people say odd things and behave in odd ways. The factors which stood out in Roger West's mind might be trifles. There was the way O'Leary had looked when he had seen the card—the kind of look a man might give if he had reason to fear the Yard. There was Billy Mulcaster's unnatural pose when he had first arrived—he hadn't rushed to his wife, but had stood there tensely, asking what West was doing, not what had happened. And the word "murder" had shaken him badly. Well it might, in the circumstances, and that by itself meant nothing. The girl's emotional outburst could be explained by her condition, and come to think, she was a bit thick at the waist. Amazingly handsome couple. Put them together on the screen and—

Forget the screen.

West had a word with the uniformed policemen, got into the car and turned toward the Mile End Road. Nearing it, he remembered something else: the size of the diamond in Rosie Mulcaster's engagement ring. It couldn't be real, of course, for it would be worth six or seven hundred pounds, and—

The Gelignite Gang had stolen tens of thousands of pounds worth of jewelry.

He drove toward the Yard, thinking of Rosie, Billy, and O'Leary, and wondering why he was allergic to O'Leary. In one way, he was relieved; a distressing job was over. He hadn't got what he had hoped to get when volunteering to take it on —that was information from Rosie Mulcaster— but it had never been more than a hope. Or just another hunch which hadn't come off. For every shot in the dark which hit the target, fifty shots missed by yards.

He turned into Mort Place, a little square not far from the docks and the Thames. The police station had a blue lamp outside it, a sergeant standing at the foot of the stairs. Several police cars were parked outside. West pulled his in to the curb and hurried toward the main entrance, nodding to the duty constable. He didn't want to stay here long, but when a Yard officer was in a district it was a sensible courtesy to call in and say "hallo" to the district superintendent. There might be several things that Sopley, the man in charge here, could do to help. Perhaps he knew O'Leary.

"Is Superintendent Sopley in?" West asked a sergeant in the charge room.

"Oh, yes, sir, expecting you, too." The sergeant smiled benignly, an aging, gray-haired man. "I'll take you up, sir." West didn't ask him how it was that Sopley was expecting him—and yet he soon found out, for Sopley was getting up from his desk, a very big man with a huge stomach, his hand outstretched.

"Hallo, Handsome, I thought you'd soon be here. Chatworth wants you to call him—better do what the Assistant Commissioner says pretty quick, eh?" Sopley motioned to a chair. "There's the telephone, help yourself."

"Thanks," West said. "There's a job you can start on for us, if you will. Check on a man named O'Leary, of 27 Nattur Street, a friend of Mulcaster, the dead man's son-in-law. O'Leary was so smooth and cocky I can't believe he's in it, but nerves catch 'em in funny ways sometimes. Then check where Mulcaster works, will you? He has a night job, too."

"Starting one of your rest cures?" Sopley asked, and grinned.

O'Leary waited in the kitchen at 28 Brickett Street, smoking a self-rolled cigarette, big hands in the pockets of his jacket. His sodden raincoat was hanging over two hooks behind the kitchen door, his hand was on the gas-stove rack. He heard movements above his head, but didn't move, although now and again he clicked his tongue with annoyance.

Billy Mulcaster started down the stairs. He came slowly. O'Leary shifted his cigarette from one side of his mouth to the other and moved nearer the door. Billy came in, smoothing down his hair. He hadn't shaved, but had brushed his hair and put on a pale gray suit of good cut; it made his shoulders seem wider than they really were. He had a freshly lit cigarette in his mouth, very white against his sallow skin. The bruise looked less angry.

"Hi," he greeted.

"How's Rosie, my boy, how is she?"

"She—she'll be all right. She don't want me to send for the doctor. I've given her a couple of aspirins, and she says she'll be all right."

"Course she will," said O'Leary. "You don't know how tough these women are, especially when a kid's on the way. Before you know where you are,

59

my lucky lad, you'll be a proud father. How you feeling yourself?"

"I—I'm all right. I—say, Mike." Billy hesitated. "Did you—did you know he was dead?" The words came out hesitatingly, as if he was not used to the idea.

O'Leary moved toward him. Slowly he closed his thick fingers round Billy's forearm. He squeezed, and then twisted slightly. He didn't hurt, just set Billy's arm in a position of tension which it would be hard to break without a lot of pain. He looked into Billy's eyes and spoke very deliberately, very softly.

"Listen to me, Billy. I didn't know, you didn't know either. We don't know a thing. I'm doing a temp'ry job at Pretzel's, helping out. We were working until three o'clock at the restaurant, get it? We were the only ones on duty, except the chef. We came straight home—you first, me afterward. I stayed the night because I didn't feel so good. That's it, that's everything. The police won't worry you or me, and they won't worry Rosie. Not if you're careful. The boss wouldn't like it if he thought you weren't going to be careful, Billy. Just tie a knot in your tongue, and remember we were working, we don't know a thing. Understand?"

Now the pressure of his fingers really hurt.

Billy didn't try to free himself. "Sure, I understand. But I didn't mean to have the—the old boy hurt. I wouldn't have done him in."

"You didn't know a thing about it," said O'Leary. "Not a damned thing. You be careful."

"I can keep my mouth shut," Billy snapped, "Why the hell can't you? Giving West all that stuff was crazy."

60

"I can handle coppers," O'Leary said. His expression suggested that he didn't like the way things had turned. "You'd better be careful, Billy. Just worry about Rosie and the kid, and forget everything else. You can take a few days off, right now. I talked to the Blower before West arrived. He said it was okay for you to look after Rosie; nice and generous nature, the Blower's got! He's worried about Rosie and he'd worried about *your* health, too, Billy." That was sly, menacing. "He's so worried, he wants me to stay and look after you, see you don't run a temperature—it wouldn't do if you was to get too hot, would it? So I'm moving in. When this is all blown over you can shift into Nattur Street, but right now you stay here. All clear, Billy?"

Billy said sharply, "I can look after myself."

"Your nerves weren't so good last night," O'Leary sneered.

"I didn't like that job last night," Billy said. "I just had a feeling about it. So what? Don't the Blower trust me?"

"He thinks two heads are better than one."

"But Rosie will wonder what the hell—"

"Never mind her," O'Leary said. "We'll find a story to satisfy our Rosie. She won't need much satisfying for a few days, anyway. I'm going to be a proper uncle to her. If that flicking cop West starts to question her again, I'm going to be around, see? We don't want the wrong things said to that swab. Just make up your mind to it, Billy, and tie that knot in your tongue. See?"

Billy said, "Yes, I see." He didn't look pleased, and his voice was flat.

O'Leary let him go and punched him playfully on the chest, as if to get back on good terms again.

"Sure you see! You're made of good stuff, Billy, you'll toughen up so that you won't recognize yourself. And in a few days, as soon as it's all over, you and Rosie can settle down to the love life again, eh? You've got a hundred nicker due from last night's job, so you're sitting pretty. You'll be able to buy Rosie—" he stopped abruptly, stumbled in his words and then grinned more broadly —"anything she wants, Billy, anything she wants. Now I'm hungry. You ever cooked bacon 'n' eggs?"

"Listen," Billy Mulcaster said in a very ugly voice, "there's just so much I'll take from anyone, the Blower, or you, or anyone else. Don't you start ordering me about. Understand?"

O'Leary looked angry, but forced a laugh.

"Okay," he said, "let's cook bacon and eggs my way!"

7

Conference

Roger West tapped at the door of the Assistant Commissioner's room two hours later and the door opened. The A.C.'s secretary, in white blouse and black skirt, prim and almost painfully efficient, greeted him with a plummy smile.

"Come in, Mr. West, Sir Guy's waiting for you."

"Thanks," Roger said. He went in briskly, taking in the group sitting round Sir Guy Chatworth's big desk. There were Cortland, a man as big and massive as Sopley of AZ Division, the Yard's senior Superintendent; lanky Beckwith, another of the Big Five, the specialist in explosives; and Chatworth sitting behind the big, flat-topped desk. Give Chatworth a white beard and a conical red hat and he could play Father Christmas to the most exacting child's satisfaction. He had grizzled hair set in tight miniature-looking curls about a tanned bald patch which glistened beneath electric light, and he had huge girth.

Lassitter, from the office of the Director of Public Prosecutions, was there too, a thin-faced, angular, acid-tongued lawyer.

Chatworth waved to a chair.

"Come along, West, sit down, we're waiting."

"Sorry, sir," Roger said, "I was delayed at AZ Division. Maitland's daughter—"

"Sir Guy, I don't want to strike a discordant note early in the discussion," Lassitter interrupted, "but I do want to try to see exactly what approach is being made to this series of crimes, and if the Chief Inspector would tell us why he thought it advisable to break the news to the victim's daughter in person, I would be grateful. It—ah—must have taken quite a lot of valuable time, and I believe that a Divisional man, normally one from the Uniformed Branch, customarily carries out this task. I appreciate the—ah—thoughtfulness, but—" He broke off, giving a thin, sardonic smile.

Chatworth said, "Why'd you tell her yourself, West?" He pushed a silver box of cigarettes across the table.

Roger took one, lit it, then spoke easily.

"Thank you, sir. There were two reasons for seeing the daughter myself. First, the personal or the human angle. I like to know the people in a case, like to get them on my side whenever it's possible. If it's someone from the Brickett Street area, that takes some doing. I reasoned that if this woman didn't exactly become a bosom friend, she wouldn't be so hostile to me as she would probably be toward a local man, uniformed or not." He smiled formally at Lassitter. "On the routine side, I confirmed that she was housekeeper to her father. I'd already concluded that the raiders had some knowledge of Maitland's likely movements. It was possible that he'd given information away, and the most likely person to say whether he had or not was his daughter."

There was a brief silence. Chatworth almost purred.

"Thank you. I fully understand." Lassitter was generous.

"What have you actually done, West?" Chatworth asked.

He would certainly want to impress the lawyer first, Roger knew, and worry about the handling of the case afterward. So Roger glanced at Chatworth's secretary, whose shorthand speed was legendary.

"It would be a great help if Miss Symes could take this down, sir; I haven't yet made out a report, and I've a crowded program." Chatworth nodded to the woman, whose book was open at a small desk at his elbow. "I was told about this murder at seven fifteen this morning by Detective Sergeant Keen at Superintendent Last's request," Roger said. "I arrived at Jefferson's department store at eight o'clock, where I interviewed Desmond Archer, the other watchman on duty last night, and a Divisional sergeant and constable. I concluded that the sergeant, Madd, was an excellent witness, the constable, Egerton, an indifferent one, the night watchman, Archer, probably unreliable. He first discovered the body, and puzzled Sergeant Madd with his excessive anxiety to make it clear that he had been on a different floor when the murder was done. After questioning, Archer admitted that he had quarreled with Maitland over Archer's desire to play a game of dominoes and Maitland's refusal."

Roger paused, to draw at his cigarette. No one spoke.

"Statements already made by Sergeant Madd and P.C. Egerton included mention of two cars, one a large American model, now established as a prewar Packard with a black or dark blue body, the other a prewar Austin which had been in the vicinity about the time of the raid on Jefferson's. I've asked the Divisions, Home Counties, and County Constabularies to look out for these cars, and when visiting AZ Division asked for a special search to be made in that vicinity.

"I've also had inquiries started about a youth named Mulcaster, Maitland's son-in-law, who was out during the night, and a friend who says he is working at the same place. Mulcaster works at Pretzel's Restaurant, by the way. Reports on both men should be in any time."

Roger paused but didn't give even a hint of a smile.

"So much for positive measures," he went on. "When I reached Jefferson's, most of the routine checking had been done, photographs had been taken, diagrams drawn. I studied the diagrams, and photographic prints should be on my desk now.

"Maitland's body had already been removed to the morgue at Pinder Street. I went to see the body and discussed the cause of death with Dr. Foreham. He thinks that blows from a blunt instrument were the cause of death—a bar of iron, possibly, certainly not a hammer. I've asked for further photographs of the wound and a further surgical and medical examination of the injuries, hoping to be able to identify the weapon more precisely.

"I also went closely into the known circumstances of the robbery, and examined the blown safes and the premises," Roger continued; and Miss Symes's pencil went inexorably on. "The safes were blown by plastic gelignite, the method adopted by the Gelignite Gang. It's the seventeenth raid of its kind in the past year—eight of them in London, nine in smaller towns within a hundred-mile radius. Department stores have been raided each time. Only silver plate, gold plate, and jewelry have been taken, except for loose cash."

Roger paused, stubbed out his cigarette, then added:

"Sir Gerald Sarkey, chairman of the board of Jefferson's, telephoned before I left for Brickett Street, and promised to have all stock records checked. His cashier, accountant, and stock controller will give this job priority until descriptions and identification marks of the stolen goods are available. Detective Sergeant Turnbull and Detective Officer Ridden are standing by. I arranged for the known numbers of the stolen treasury notes to be circulated to banks, travel agencies, police stations, and *bureaux de change*."

Miss Symes's pencil lead snapped. With scarcely a pause, she produced a sharpened pencil from a pocket in her skirt.

"There's evidence that sacks were filled at the safes and carried or dragged up to the ground floor, then to another staircase and down through to a basement site next door," Roger said. "A car or van was used to take the loot away. A hole had been made in the basement wall during the day, under cover of a gas-main repair, and only loosely filled in. All of our men who might be able to help identify the daytime workers have been alerted."

Roger checked the flood of words again.

Cortland was openly grinning; Chatworth relaxed; Beckwith fiddled with his watch chain. Only Lassitter kept a poker face.

"Anything more?" Chatworth asked mildly.

"We warned all trade channels to whom the stolen goods might be offered," Roger declared, "but I fancy it'll be as sticky as always. Only a few trifles have been recovered up and down the country."

Now Lassitter rubbed his long fingers together.

"In other words you aren't too optimistic."

"When you've been working for the better part of a year on one case, co-operating with nine county police forces and using every trick the Yard has, you don't expect to find an easy way," Roger said. "The thing that surprises me is the murder. Once before they trussed up a night watchman, but didn't hurt him. This murder could have been unintentional, of course, but—" He shrugged.

"Go on," Chatworth said.

"Maitland was struck from behind. There seem to have been very few blows. You don't hit a man hard enough to crush his skull unless you intend to hurt him badly."

Big Cortland broke in. "Could mean they're using a different crew." He appeared to ruminate. "Or else that another gang is using the same methods."

"You've been to Jefferson's, Beckwith," Chatworth remarked.

Beckwith said, "West was right first time. Same crew, same methods, same kind of plastic gelignite, same kind of hessian sacks, too—picked up a few strands of hessian from one of the safes; a sack caught in a lock. That's the third lot of sacks. Twenty-seven million of those sacks were manufactured last year," he added, with a swift glance under his eyebrows at Lassitter. "Still, we're keeping at the manufacturers and the chief buyers and all wholesalers."

"I see, yes," Lassitter said, and his fingers rubbed again. "The matter of the disposal of the stolen goods, now, isn't that peculiar? They make some big—uh—hauls. I don't know whether you know the value of the goods stolen in these seventeen robberies, but—" he took a slip of paper out of his pocket, unfolded it, and adjusted his horn-rimmed glasses—"very nearly two—"

"Insured value up to last night, one hundred and eighty-three thousand pounds, eleven shillings and five pence," Roger put in.

Lassitter's head jerked up.

"Exactly right, I—" He raised his hands, gave a little laugh, like ice in a thick glass. "I stand rebuked, Chief Inspector. I hope you will be given the assignment if anyone should ever murder me."

"I can't imagine you ever giving cause," Roger murmured.

Lassitter started, then chuckled almost warmly.

"There's one other factor which might be significant," Roger went on, in the much easier atmosphere, "but it's difficult to get at the real truth. It's about Sir Gerald Sarkey and Jefferson's as a whole."

That sparked everyone's interest.

"Really," remarked Lassitter. "In what way?"

"We've done some close checking on the Gelignite Gang's robberies," Roger told them mildly. "Two or three peculiar facts emerged. In most cases, the robberies were staged after one-day lightning sales, as the Jefferson organization calls them. They've become very popular up and down the country. The local press carries a splash advertisement the night before, a few special lines are offered very cheap, the crowd comes, and takings in all departments shoot up. Of the seventeen robberies, thirteen followed such one-day sales."

No one looked away from Roger.

"The other jobs were on the night before staff paydays, when a lot of ready money was lying about anyhow," he went on. "Much bigger hauls were made than you'd expect if it were just luck. It looked as if they spied out the ground carefully beforehand—or had a spy in Jefferson's."

Lassitter murmured, "Very interesting, but I don't quite see how this affects Sir Gerald Sarkey."

"I think you will, very soon. We already knew that the thieves went to a lot of trouble to find out what precautions were taken, the number of the night staff and that kind of information, and we knew that the timing of the raids had always been good. So we looked for common factors to each of the burgled stores. All of them are in the Jefferson group, although eleven are only financially controlled by Jefferson's—or Sir Gerald Sarkey—and Sarkey doesn't appear on the list of directors. He's chairman of the board of a controlling company, however, and kingpin of them all."

"Well, what then?" Chatworth was almost sharp.

"So we checked on Sarkey himself." Roger coughed suddenly, and took several seconds to recover, and each man waited on his next words.

"So—sorry, sir. It proved to be worth doing. Sir Gerald Sarkey has had some personal bother in the past nine or twelve months—approximately over the period of the department-store robberies."

Lassitter sat upright. "Well, well."

"There have been two small burglaries at Sarkey's Sunningdale home," Roger said. "The first was reported to the police, the second wasn't. I wondered why he should want to hush up a burglary. He has received at least three abusive and threatening letters in the same period—"

"Sure about their character?" Chatworth demanded.

"Our informant about this is his private secretary, a Miss Caroline Wellesley," Roger told him. "She's a middle-aged woman with a full sense of responsibility, and is worried and upset by the situation. She told us this in confidence—she read the letters which Sarkey kept in his desk. By 'us' I mean a detective officer named Ridden, who did a very good job." He gave that time to sink in. "There've been other incidents, too. Once, when he was stepping into his car, a firework exploded under Sarkey's feet, ignited by the movement as he got in. When all these things are added up, sir, they look like a campaign against Sir Gerald. The significant thing is that they are concurrent with the Gelignite Gang raids."

Lassitter said, "I am more reassured than I thought I could possibly be. You'll keep me informed, won't you?"

He left soon afterward, and the atmosphere became almost carefree. Chatworth positively beamed as he lit a cheroot.

"Anything else up your sleeve?" he demanded.

"I want a go at Sir Gerald Sarkey," Roger said promptly. "He's a bit autocratic, though—didn't like it when I couldn't promise to meet him at the store at ten o'clock."

"Wasn't exactly hurrying, was he?" Chatworth asked.

"He lives out at Sunningdale and couldn't get to town earlier," Roger explained. "I'll see him as soon as I can."

"Take your own time," advised Chatworth, "and don't take too much from the gentleman."

There were two urgent things to do.

One: find out everything possible about Sir Gerald Sarkey, his family, his financial affairs, his reputation in the city.

Two: go over all reports of robberies from the big department stores, check everything that had been recovered, try to trace it back to a single source.

Roger preferred to try the personal angle himself, wanting to know all he could about Sarkey before he met him. He put a sergeant on to the other job, and sat at his desk with three telephones in front of him for an intensive half hour. If there was a short cut to the kind of information he wanted, it would be through the newspapers; and most newspapers had a soft spot for Handsome West as well as hope for future favors.

He called the *Globe*.

"Sarkey? Sure, we've a big file on him," the *Globe* news editor said. "Wait till I send for it." There were background murmurs. "Of course, you know about his son Philip."

"Pretend I don't know a thing," Roger said.

He could almost see the *Globe* man's grin.

"I don't even have to pretend! Philip Sarkey's the motor-racing ace. Hell bent for heaven if anyone ever was, he takes the craziest risks. Fine driver, there isn't a better. That's when he races, mind you. He doesn't do much these days, and rumor has it that there was a tremendous fight with his old man. Sarkey's a widower, and Philip his son and heir—he didn't want a broken-necked heir."

"So Philip knuckled under," Roger mused.

"He knew which side his bread was buttered," the *Globe* man declared. "Sarkey kicked one son out on his neck with the proverbial shilling—don't think I'm the original memory man, I've got the file in front of me and it's all coming back. Lemme see.... Yes, son number one was named Reginald. Expelled, sent down, mixed with dopeys, suspected of rifling papa's safe. hard drinker, lots of little Reginalds all over the place to many a fair maid's sorrow—mind if I get lyrical?"

"You're doing fine." Roger grinned.

"I want priority next time you get a murder on your hands, mind you." The *Globe* man was turning papers over; Roger could hear them. "Hm, yes. Reginald was all that and more. Source of information: an old family servant who was pensioned off after Sarkey's wife died. Like her name?"

"Please."

"Elizabeth Carter, who—no go, though, here's a note that she died last year. But the stuff's all vetted, Handsome, and vetoed, too. Our Old Man is a pal of the great Sarkey, and we'll never be allowed to use this unless they have a row."

"How long ago was this Reginald cut off?" Roger asked, and found himself wondering what manner of man could really cast off his own flesh and blood.

"Sixteen years ago," the *Globe* man said promptly. "The present heir, Philip, was only nine. Sarkey's wife died the following year."

"Anything heard of Reginald since?"

"Said to have gone abroad."

"Said?"

"You have to do something yourself," the *Globe* man protested plaintively. "I can't be sure, we were never able to trace him. Now lemme see— Philip's got a Mayfair flat, he doesn't live with the old man out at Sunningdale. Said to be soft over an unofficial niece—the old man's!—named Barbara Denny. Blue blood and all that, late thirties, daughter of old family friends, works at Jefferson's as welfare officer."

"Reputation?" asked Roger.

"Unblemished."

Roger chuckled.

"Wait until she meets you!" He ran his eyes over the notes he had made. "If you do find anything else about the lost son, let me know, will you?"

"Yes. What's it all about, Handsome?"

"As soon as I dare, I'll tell you," Roger promised.

He rang off, studied the notes again, decided that he need not try another press contact, and called Chatworth. He had to hold on. While he did so, the door of his office opened and the sergeant who was checking the stolen goods which had been recovered came in with a sheaf of papers. Roger pointed to a chair opposite him. The sergeant lowered himself cautiously; a big man. Still holding on, Roger said:

"Let's have it."

"Not much to have," the sergeant declared, and put papers on the desk. "These came from dozens of different places—pawnbrokers, secondhand shops, and small jewelers all over the country. Every report's the same. The stuff was bought off a cove who'd never been in the shop before, with a spiel about bankrupt stocks. He never sold more than a hundred quid's worth or so to any one place. The stuff was all new, and it sounded genuine. Got a dozen different descriptions of the man who sold it—they tally more or less, could be the same man as seen by different shopkeepers. You know how it is."

"Don't I," Roger said resignedly.

The sergeant stood up. "There's one thing. Sometimes there were two men, in an old Packard."

Roger flashed, "That's our line. Get a general call out for reports on old Packards, go right after this car, and hurry. I—"

Chatworth's voice suddenly boomed, "What is it now?"

By the time Roger had reported and rung off, the sergeant had gone. Roger looked about the office, where five desks, all bilious yellow in color and brightly varnished, stood with a small armchair and an upright chair by the side of them, a swivel desk chair behind each. Two other C.I.'s looked up, and one said:

"Hallo, Handsome, having a nice time?"

Roger looked through some handwritten notes on his desk; most were about other jobs, three simply told him that the things he had put in hand were moving. There was no news except that a P.C. from the Central London Division, who heard about the Jefferson job before going off duty, reported that he had seen a big Austin, prewar model, stop outside a restaurant in Ash Street, Soho. Pity it wasn't a Packard.

But as he studied this, hope that was nearly excitement began to rise, for the restaurant was *the Pretzel*. It opened only for the evening, and was often open as late as half-past two and three o'clock. It catered chiefly for revelers at big functions which ended late, and it had a good reputation for food, especially Belgian and northern French cooking. Roger knew it; so did Chatworth.

And Billy Mulcaster and O'Leary worked there.

The big Austin had been parked outside for ten minutes or more, and the P.C. who reported this had seen it in Ash Street half a dozen times before.

Talking to Sarkey would have to wait. Roger grabbed the telephone again.

"Sergeants' Room," he said, and held on. Then: "West here. Find all the dope you can on the Pretzel Restaurant, Ash Street, as quickly as you can, will you? No need to break your neck. Have a word with the Division if it will help, but get everything. I hope to be back here by two."

A sergeant said, "Right, sir."

Roger went briskly downstairs to the room where the newspapermen were waiting for tidbits of information as well as real news from the Back Room Inspector, who fed them as best he could.

Roger went into the Inspector's office.

"Mind if I have a word with them, Jim?"

"No wonder you get a better press than the rest of us put together," the Back Room Inspector said. "Okay, go ahead."

There were fifteen men in the room beyond, with telephones, desks, a litter of newspapers, and a fug of smoke. At sight of West, they jumped up as one man; two reporters at the telephone slammed the receivers down.

"I'm in the usual hurry, but you chaps can do us a favor," Roger said. "Get your reports a little confused, will you? Was Maitland killed instantaneously, or was he alive when found? Actually, he was dead, but—"

Two or three men said, "We'll fix it."

"Thanks. I don't know if any of you saw Lassiter, but he was here. Home Office very anxious is your line! But don't take a smack at him, he means well!"

"Hal-*lo*! High pressure?"

"They only want results. After all, seventeen robberies and not a single arrest. If you care to quote me from here on—'We've been hammering at this job for a long time, and cracks are showing.'"

Two men were already at the telephones. Others rushed to them as Roger finished, "That's all I dare give you, now," and went out to a kind of chorus of thanks.

The *Globe* would have its special reward later.

Roger allowed himself ten minutes for a cup of coffee and a cigarette in the canteen, which was practically deserted, then went out to his car. Something yellow caught his eye, tacked down by the seat, and he fished out a small pencil. One end was badly sharpened, the other end bitten down. Richard was the pencil biter. Roger slipped it into his pocket, smiled, and drove off.

He found himself thinking of the boys. Richard's tears, Scoopy's question. What made men bad? What made a man a killer? He tried to shake off the gloom which the recollection brought, but it

77

wouldn't go completely. What had made Rosie Mulcaster hysterical? What had caused her husband's theatrical appearance?

And there was O'Leary.

He turned into Oxford Street, which was thronged with people and thick with traffic. Jefferson's looked no different from what it did any day of the week. Its big double doors kept opening and closing, people streamed in and out, the windows lured the passers-by. Jefferson's was almost a national institution, and Sir Gerald Sarkey, who had taken the store over twenty years before when it had nearly gone bankrupt, was the genius who had made it so.

Roger turned out of Oxford Street. There was no room to park. He had to drive round the block twice before he squeezed into a vacant spot, and it was several minutes' walk away from the store. In the side street, a little crowd of people had gathered to gape; police kept moving them on. The man on door duty recognized Roger.

"Morning, Mr. West."

"Hallo, there." Roger smiled briefly and went in. He had to wait for the lift, standing among a crowd of women shoppers, not a man among them. Outstanding was a tall woman who had a quality hard to define but which made her quite distinct from all the others. She wore a beautifully tailored suit of deep yellow color—Richard's pencil without the polish. Beneath this she wore a dark green blouse, high at the neck, and with cuffs showing. Her small hat was little more than an inverted saucer—and all the decoration her lovely chestnut hair needed. She wasn't so much beautiful as striking—her nose was high-bridged, her eyes gray with flecks of amber, clear and intelligent. Her complexion was good, her make-up wasn't overdone. Her mouth reminded him of Janet's—full, nicely shaped, generous, and easy to smile—he could see that as she smiled at a baby in the arms of a flustered-looking woman in a brown coat. The tall woman was distinctive enough to take Roger's mind off the problem for a few moments; to make him forget to plan his approach to Sarkey.

The lift arrived.

It was nearly full when only Roger and the tall woman were left outside.

"Sorry to have kept you, miss," said the one-armed lift attendant. The woman stepped forward. "Sorry, sir, next car please."

The woman looked at Roger. "I'm so sorry."

"It's quite all right." He smiled. It hadn't been much of an encounter, but it had raised his spirits. Little things often did. Good-looking women who stood out from a crowd didn't grow on trees.

The next lift came almost at once; he couldn't have been two minutes behind the first. When they reached the seventh and top floor, where the offices were, he was alone.

He went straight to Sir Gerald Sarkey's office, which he'd seen that morning, with the word CHAIRMAN painted in gilt on the door of a wood which looked like walnut. He tapped, and a girl called, "Come in." Miss Symes's double, also in black and white, looked up from a large desk. This was Miss Caroline Wellesley, who had talked, worriedly, to a Yard man, but had not met Roger before.

The desk was immaculate. The room was large,

carpeted, expensive-looking, with easy chairs, cigarettes, magazines, and some effective modern
paintings on the wall.

"Good morning."

"I'm afraid I'm late," Roger said. "I'm Chief Inspector West."

"Oh, yes, sir. Sir Gerald asked me to let you go
straight in." She stood up, tapped at another door,
and opened it.

A man was saying in a rather affected voice:

"My dear Barbara, I don't understand your concern for this girl. I think you should impose limits
on your charity." He glanced at the door. "Yes, Miss
Wellesley?"

"Chief Inspector West, Sir Gerald."

Quickly, smoothly, unpleasantly, Sarkey said,
"So he has found time to come after all. If you care
to stay, Barbara, you may learn everything you
want to know."

Roger, already in the room, saw Sarkey sitting
at a huge, highly polished desk, a well-preserved
sixtyish, thin, sharp-featured, not undistinguished
in his way. He was immaculate in black and white,
iron-gray hair was brushed sleekly back from his
forehead, thin and colorless lips were set.

Standing by the desk was the woman who had
come up in the first lift.

8

Sir Gerald Sarkey

There was a quick flash of recognition, and then the woman moved back. Sarkey looked up at Roger coldly. He didn't get up, didn't offer his hand, but stared straight into Roger's eyes. He was hostile—coldly, unmistakably. Undoubtedly he expected Roger to wilt, to avoid his gaze. Roger stood quite still, unsmiling, unspeaking, while the silence dragged out noticeably. Sarkey's lips tightened still more; he began to feel the sense of strain.

Roger judged his moment.

"Good morning, Sir Gerald," he said. "I'm sorry about the burglary, and very sorry indeed about the night watchman."

Silence again—

Sarkey did not quite know how to react, seemed surprised by the approach. He glanced quickly at the woman, then stood up.

"Good morning, Chief Inspector. Yes, it's a bad business. This is Miss Barbara Denny. Barbara, this is Chief Inspector West you've doubtless heard so much about."

Roger smiled and bowed slightly to the woman, saw the flash of a smile in her eyes, knew that Sarkey had, in effect, climbed down; if they were going to get on terms, this was the chance.

"How are you, Miss Denny? I'm sorry I was held up; the Assistant Commissioner has taken a keenly personal interest in this job."

"Indeed," said Sarkey, dryly. "Sit down, Chief Inspector. I think Miss Denny is anxious for a little information before we get on with our business."

The woman, now sitting down, gave a quick smile that suggested that her lips were the true guide to her temperament. Her voice was nicely pitched.

"Sir Gerald doesn't quite approve, Chief Inspector, but I would like to go and see Jem Maitland's daughter. She used to work here before she was married, and was very popular. Have you seen her?" She spoke as if she knew that he had.

"Yes."

"Was she very upset?"

"Very upset indeed," Roger said. His smile had the quality which had helped Rosie. "I wouldn't go and see her by yourself, and I wouldn't go just yet. Later in the day, perhaps, or tomorrow."

Sarkey looked approval.

"Why wouldn't you go by yourself?" Barbara Denny asked.

Roger found himself rooting for a cigarette. Sarkey pushed a box toward him with a murmured invitation. The girl had an imperious air about her now; in her way she was as used to command as Sarkey, and she wouldn't easily take no for an answer.

Roger gave a hesitant laugh, hinting at embarrassment he didn't really feel.

"I suppose the honest answer is that I don't think you'll like the neighborhood! And unless you choose your time, you could run into trouble. We still have black spots, and Brickett Street is in the center of one of them. It might amount to nothing more than a few wolf whistles and some insolence, and there might be nothing at all."

"Perhaps you'll escort me yourself," Barbara Denny said, almost tartly.

"I'll be happy to."

She was surprised into a laugh. "Then you must let me know when you're going to see Rosie again! I intend to go sometime today. You won't leave it too late, will you?" She stood up, and there was open defiance in her manner as she looked at Sarkey. "I'll be in my office, Gerald."

"Very well," Sarkey said.

The woman reached the door, taking long, easy strides, graceful as a woman could be. Then she turned.

"I should hate you to think that this is idle curiosity, Chief Inspector. I am interested in the welfare of the staff, and so I'm affected both personally and officially both by Maitland's death and his daughter's grief. And"—all her pose vanished—"I would really like to help her."

She went out.

Sarkey said, "I'd be grateful if you can make an opportunity to take Miss Denny to this house, Chief Inspector. Now, before I send for your man Turnbull and the heads of the departments, who should have the information you require by this time, I would like a word with you semi-officially."

He was as relaxed as he was ever likely to be, yet his manner was aloof; it had been with Barbara Denny and probably was with everyone. "This is the seventeenth raid—successful and costly raid—on stores under my control. The daring of last night's burglary—as well as the death of the night watchman—give me very great cause for alarm. I want you to know that I shall look for early results, and shall want to know the reason why if they don't come."

He didn't smile.

Roger said formally. "So shall all of us at the Yard, including the Assistant Commissioner, Sir Gerald. None of us enjoys being balked. The Gelignite Gang hasn't done the Yard any good and hasn't helped any of us who're working on it. You couldn't be more anxious for results than we are. Do you follow newspaper reports of crimes?"

Sarkey was taken aback by this sudden change of ground.

"I read the *Times* and the *Telegraph*—"

"You'd find more reports of the kind I mean in the popular dailies," Roger said easily. "The *Record* picked up a thing last week which worries us. The Gelignite Gang itself has got away with these seventeen raids; as a result, a lot of little crooks are showing more daring in blowing safes and strongrooms. The jobs aren't all connected, and most are very clumsy, but not all the rogues are caught, and the more who get away, the more follow their example. Once we break this gang, we'll send a lot of imitators scuttling. Add that to murder, and we're really on our toes."

Sarkey looked at him for a long time before a

hint of a smile began to play at the corners of the pale, well-marked lips.

"I'm glad that you also have a strong motive for wanting to find the raiders, Chief Inspector. I shall do everything I can to help. Is there anything you would like to say to me before I send for the others?"

"I don't think so."

Sarkey pressed a bell push fitted to the side of his desk. If he had secret fears, he concealed them well.

Detective Sergeant Turnbull was a big, lionlike animal of a man, very confident, quite unable to suffer fools gladly. He came in with Jefferson's chief accountant and the controller of stocks, the buyer of the jewelry-and-plate department, and the cashier. He had sheaves of notes and lists of identification numbers, and was full of what he had done. A preliminary list of bank-note numbers was already in circulation; some of the lists of jewels and silverware were already being typed.

When the men had gone, Roger said, "I think I can leave this end to Turnbull, Sir Gerald. I'll keep an eye on it myself, of course."

Sarkey raised no objection.

Archer, the other night watchman, was dressed in a well-pressed suit of navy blue when he sat in Roger's office with his bowler hat on his knees, looking scared and miserable. He didn't alter his story, and kept saying that he didn't feel it was on his conscience—if Maitland had listened to him he would have been playing dominoes and the

85

murder wouldn't have happened. But the police wouldn't have to tell Jefferson's that, would they?

"If the police have their way, Jefferson's will double the night staff from now on," Roger said. "All right, Archer. Going on duty tonight?"

"Oh, yes."

"Needn't worry about lightning striking twice in the same place," Roger said. "Not that kind of lightning, anyhow."

He made a quick estimate of the time desk work would keep him in the office, then put in a call to Jefferson's and was put through to Miss Barbara Denny promptly. If this needed justification, he could say that the second trip to Brickett Street was a move toward making Sir Gerald Sarkey better disposed. "Oh, Miss Denny, it's West here." She didn't say. "Who?" or sound puzzled. "I can be free at five o'clock, if that will suit you."

"Perfectly, thank you very much."

"Glad to help," Roger said, "and I've a feeling that Rosie will need it. Good-by."

He rang off, and could picture her standing out among the other women by the lift, with that sleek yellow suit. It was now a little after three. He put the thought of her out of his mind, and started going through reports, mostly about other jobs, charges pending, the next morning's police court hearings, the mass of detail which never seemed to be quite up to date. It was quiet in the office. A coal fire burned sluggishly to supplement the indifferent central heating. It was warm enough for him to work with his coat off and the ends of his tie hanging down.

Soon he was studying lists of stolen goods. Apart from the money, mostly in one-pound and ten-shilling notes of unknown serial numbers, it was all jewelry, silver, silver plate, and cutlery: just the kind of goods any jeweler would have in stock.

Where goods had been found, the makers' trademarks had been obliterated skillfully and others superimposed. It was expert work from beginning to end, and the stolen goods could sell, without suspicion, in almost any jeweler's or big store. By supplying in small lots, the distributors showed a lot of cunning.

Sopley came through, laconically. O'Leary was working at the Pretzel Restaurant, as a temporary kitchen hand; Billy Mulcaster was a waiter at the same place. It would be some time before their story could be checked.

The Pretzel was high on the list for further inquiries.

At half-past four, Roger pushed the papers away from him, tightened his tie, poked his fingers through his hair, and stood up. He'd better get off to Jefferson's. Barbara Denny might be a woman with a heart, but she wouldn't like being kept waiting.

He was looking forward to going with her, too. Instinctively, he felt that they would get along. Her interest in Rosie was almost certainly genuine, and she would be anxious to help. One aspect which needed pointing up much more clearly was that of Sarkey's personal bothers, about which he had been so reticent. There were several good reasons why an hour or so with Barbara Denny would do no harm.

Roger stood up.

The telephone bell rang.

"West speaking."

"Handsome, we're on the move!" It was the bull-like voice of Turnbull, who had been at Jefferson's. "Just looked in at Central Division. They've found that Austin, parked near the Pretzel Restaurant, Ash Street. It belongs to the chef, man named Hick. And he—"

"Take it easy! It might have been borrowed."

"I don't care whether it was begged, borrowed, or stolen," Turnbull roared. "Some bits of hessian were in the trunk, made from the same kind of sacking as that used to carry the loot away. What's more, we found a small diamond with the hessian, dislodged from a ring or something. Shall I have a word with Hick or wait for you?"

"I'm on my way," Roger said. "Hold everything, but have the place watched."

He didn't remember Barbara Denny until he was halfway toward Ash Street, held up in a narrow street jammed with traffic because one side was lined with parked cars. He ought to have telephoned and postponed his visit. He could use the radio, but wouldn't that be making rather too much of it? It would be better to telephone from the restaurant—she wouldn't have left yet; it still wasn't five o'clock.

Then Roger turned into Ash Street and forgot everything but the scene there.

A policeman was falling like a log, another standing in statuelike poise with a hand to his mouth, and a man racing away from a doorway near the policeman.

Roger jammed on his brakes and the engine stalled. He flung open the door and jumped out.

The tires of a van behind him squealed, and the driver put a hand on his horn. It blared. Other

88

sounds were audible above the screech. A high, piercing note of a police whistle, and a roar in a stentorian voice; also, in a pause in the blaring, the sharp sound of the footsteps of running men.

The man Roger had seen rushing out of the shop doorway was only fifty yards away, visible between the parked cars, and turning to look over his shoulder. Roger ran between two cars and reached the pavement while the man was still twenty feet or so away.

He carried a gun.

9

The Pretzel Restaurant

The man was youthful and moving fast, with his left arm swinging and his right hand held up, pointing the gun. As Roger saw him, he was looking over his shoulder toward a policeman already on the move. Then he turned and saw Roger.

Less than ten feet separated them.

Roger swayed to one side, feinting. The man moved the same way, with a body swerve which could only have been learned on a football or hockey field. Check. The gun leveled. Roger held his hands out, his feet wide apart, and stared into pale eyes. He sensed the decision to shoot, and the range was deadly. Fear, thought, experience, and reflexes worked as one. He plunged forward, his hands outstretched toward the man's ankles. He heard the roar of a shot but felt no pain, and nothing hit him. He caught the polished toe of a shoe, his left hand slid under the raised foot; then the man's full weight came down on it. Pain pierced through Roger, and he gasped aloud.

He sensed the man leaping over him.

Gritting his teeth, the pain in his hand so bad that it nearly drove him silly, Roger staggered to his feet. He balked the constable, who hesitated, missed a step, and then fell heavily against a plate-glass window. It boomed like thunder. The policeman looked foolish, his mouth open, cheeks flushed, helmet nearly off and whistle hanging on its bright chain from a tunic pocket.

"After him," breathed Roger.

He turned round. A kind of desperation gave him the strength to go on, although his hand couldn't have felt worse if he'd jagged it in a band saw. He staggered, until his head cleared and he managed to run. Everything had happened in a few bewildering seconds; the fugitive was not at the corner, coattails flying. As Roger started to run, the man turned the corner.

The policeman, no fool, grabbed his whistle; the blast screeched above the traffic.

Roger reached the corner where Ash Street met Green Street, which was the wider. Cars were parked on either side. A few people were standing in shop doorways or on the pavement, gaping. Everyone had heard the whistle. A car engine roared. The man in brown still ran, and Roger saw him turn round again, the gun raised. He didn't fire; perhaps he thought that Roger was too far away. He pounded on.

A middle-aged woman stepped out of a shop, into his path.

She screamed.

The man with the gun swung his left arm desperately, struck her breast-high, and sent her reeling back into the shop, arms waving, feet kicking as she fell. Further along were two women, one of as she fell. Further along were two women, one of them pushing a pram, a man by himself and, beyond them, a policeman running this way with his whistle shrilling.

The pram was in the fugitive's path.

Roger saw the woman stop, open her mouth, then push the pram desperately against a shop window. But there was still hardly room for the fugitive to pass. The approaching policeman was nearer him, while the one behind Roger had turned the corner and was thumping along.

The fugitive turned sharply and fired at Roger, a wild, senseless shot. The bullet struck a plate-glass window, which broke with an explosive roar.

It drowned the sound of a car engine.

Roger saw the fugitive jump off the pavement between two of the parked cars. Roger did the same, twenty yards or so behind. As he stepped out of the line of cars onto the road, he foresaw everything that was going to happen with a sense of awful inevitability. It made him forget his own danger, his trampled hand, his hopes of making a capture. He was moving too fast to stop running, but grabbed at the wing of a car to check his progress.

A horn blared on a high, frightening note.

A big, sleek car, an open sports model, was coming along the road. The fugitive was jumping desperately toward the other side. Nothing in the world could save him. When the awful truth dawned on him, he seemed hypnotized, and actually checked his movement. Tires squealed as the brakes were jammed on but they could only check the speed; the car couldn't stop. The driver, a young man with black hair and a pale face, looked like a gargoyle.

Then the car hit the fugitive.

Roger heard the crunching sound, and saw the man flung downward. Squealing tires and squealing brakes merged in a hideous cacophony. Something splashed on Roger's sound hand, something else splashed on his cheek. The car, pushing the mangled body, swerved to one side and came to a standstill, with what was left of the man in brown beneath the car.

The driver still looked like a gargoyle, staring open mouthed, eyes dark with horror.

Then all noises stopped except those far away; all footsteps ceased. A dozen men and three women stared at what lay in the road amid a silence which was like an epitaph. Suddenly, a man close to the woman with the pram pitched forward in a dead faint, and, feeling him brush against her legs, the woman cried out.

Roger saw nothing of this, but fought against the nausea which the sight in the road caused. He gritted his teeth and went forward. His left hand was burning from the middle joints downward, but it was no longer excruciating pain. He saw two policemen's helmets beyond the parked cars, but he was nearest. His mind began to work again, and he raised his head and called out sharply:

"Get back to the restaurant. Hurry!" He began to move fast, reached the side of the car's driver, and saw the man licking his lips. "Listen," he said, "he was running away from me, you hadn't a chance. You just hadn't a chance, understand." He put a card into the man's hand and went on roughly:

"Jerk out of it! Show that to the police, just tell the truth." He swung away in time to see other men hurrying forward, one a policeman who hadn't heard his order, or else didn't know what restaurant he meant. This man could deal with the horrified driver.

Roger started to run back to Ash Street, but soon slackened his pace. By the time he reached the corner he was walking, and looking at his left hand. The fingers were grazed and a nail was badly split, but he could move the joints, and there wasn't much blood. One round spot, like a blot of red ink, was on his wrist.

A car came along from the other direction, and Roger saw Turnbull getting out, with two other men presumably from Central Division. Turnbull was going into the restaurant when a uniformed policeman, who arrived at the same time, spoke to him. He looked along the road and saw Roger.

He didn't speak.

Roger said, "Hallo. You timed it better than I did. Send a man to Green Street; tell him to go with the ambulance when it comes for the mess." He didn't know that he looked as pale as the driver of the sports car, and that his voice had a rasping note.

"Right," said Turnbull, and turned to one of the men who had come with him. "Hear that?... Thanks, I'll be glad if you will." He didn't ask questions, but took a flask out of his pocket, then gripped Roger's arm and took him into the Pretzel Restaurant. "Take a nip of this," he said. "I'll find out what happened."

The flask contained brandy.

Roger wanted to go with Turnbull and two other men, one of them in uniform, but knew that he wasn't in good enough shape. Five minutes' rest would help him a lot. He held his hand up because it throbbed when he let it hang down. The brandy was already doing him good. He didn't like the picture of what he had seen, but it could have been worse; only the fugitive gunman had been hurt.

"Hurt!"

But hadn't a policeman fallen?

Roger heard a man just outside the door, on the pavement.

He was standing in a small entrance hall, with a notice saying CLOAKROOM just by him, and a recess with two or three rows of pegs and a counter with a roll of pink cloakroom tickets. He could see the corner of a small bar, and, beyond a curtain which was pulled back, could also see several tables laid for dinner, glasses and cutlery glittering.

The man outside said, "What's up?" The voice was familiar but Roger couldn't place it. The tone was truculent, and that of a policeman who answered was flat and tired.

"There's been a bit of bother. What do you want?"

"I work here," the other man said. "I think—" Then he stopped. "Okay, okay, I'll wait till it's all over, I don't want to run into no trouble." There were a grunt and a pause, followed by footsteps.

That voice was irritatingly familiar, but Roger couldn't place it. He moved toward the door, opened it, and saw at least forty people gathered in a semicircle about the restaurant and one man pushing his way through as if very anxious to get away.

He wore a shapeless raglan raincoat, which looked damp, and a green pork-pie hat. When he was among the crowd, he turned to look round.

It was O'Leary.

There wasn't time to send a man after O'Leary; Roger couldn't go himself, and wasn't sure that he wanted to alarm the man yet. But he felt much better; rather as if he'd had a long sleep. This was one of the breaks which always came sooner or later, and O'Leary wasn't likely to be a difficult man to find. The AZ Division was already checking him. There would be another report before the night was out.

Turnbull had gone through the restaurant.

Roger pushed the curtains aside and went in the same direction. A door at the far end was closed, but voices sounded, and Roger reached the door and pushed it open without announcing his arrival. His left elbow was bent and he lodged the stinging fingers inside his coat—and watched and listened.

Half a dozen men, most of them in aprons, one wearing a chef's tall cap and two of them with coats off and wearing dark trousers and suspenders, stood by a long, gas-cooking range. Two other men, in blue aprons, were by a huge sink, where there were piles of scraped carrots, peeled potatoes, fresh spinach, green beans, a dozen other oddments. Turnbull was talking to the bigger of the two chefs, an ungainly, uncouth-looking man with a curiously indifferent manner. His mouth hung open a little; his eyelids were heavy and drooped over his eyes, which looked dull, lackluster.

Turnbull said, "Well, who was he?"

"I told you," the chef said. "I'm in charge just now. We've had staff trouble, and the boss is away ill. So I do every damned thing. Last week this chap wanted a job, so I gave him a job. Waiter. Today it was his turn to clean silver, and he was due here at three o'clock. And he cleaned the silver." The chef's voice was toneless and his manner indifferent. All the other men watched him, and the Central Division officer who had come with Turnbull was watching them in turn.

"What was his name?" Turnbull demanded.

"Dillon, Pat Dillon."

"What did he use for references?"

"Listen," said the big chef, "a man asks me for a job, I like the look of him so I give him a job, I don't ask for references. His name's Dillon and we've a record of his address and maybe his insurance card, I don't know if he'd brought it in already. So that's all. And I've got to get dinner for a party at half-past six, so will you get out of my kitchen?"

Turnbull was known to be hot-tempered.

"Oh, yes," he said sarcastically, "just as soon as we know why Dillon had a gun, and—"

"I wouldn't know."

The constable said, "Excuse me, sir, I know what happened. I had a request from a patrol car to keep an eye on this restaurant, and was walking up and down outside in Ash Street, sir. There's a side entrance—couple of houses next door was bombed, that's why—and I went and had a look there, to make sure no one got out without being seen and described, sir. They were my orders. This man Dillon was looking out of the side door. When he saw me, he ducked inside. Two other officers had arrived by then, sir, so they went round to the front and I stayed at the side. Dillon shot at them, and then ran—he wounded Constable Sheridan in the shoulder, but not seriously. That's all, sir."

Turnbull had been watching the big, uncouth chef.

"Thanks. Did you take this man on yourself, Mr. Hicks?"

"I'm in charge," the chef repeated as he scratched his chin. "Listen, it's an important party and they're going to the theater afterward."

Roger moved forward, slowly.

"We don't want to make things more difficult than they have to be," he said. "We can talk to you when you're not so busy. Sergeant Turnbull, have a good look round will you, especially in the cellar and the wine bins, the vegetable racks and the cold-storage room or the deep freeze, whatever they use. Everywhere, in fact." He winked at Turnbull. "And if you, Mr. Hicks—"

"No 's.' Why should you search our place?"

"Because a man who worked here tried to shoot some policemen. It'll take ten minutes to get a warrant—you might as well save us the trouble."

The big chef stared straight at Roger. His eyes were a little brighter under the heavy lids, and he looked as if he was going to get angry. But he didn't, and his voice maintained the same flat tone.

"Okay, but make it quick."

"We will. When can you spare me ten minutes?"

"Oh, save me from flickin' coppers," said Hick disgustedly. "Louis, you get things started, I'll see what I can do to get the gentlemen satisfied." He turned without enthusiasm to Roger. "There's an office upstairs, come and talk there. Not that I can help you."

The office was on the first floor, small, well kept, with a big safe in one corner, steel filing cabinets, and three telephones.

"We got a bug business," the uncouth man said. "We do inside catering here and we do outside catering and we make money. The boss being sick makes it hard, but—"

"Where is he?"

"Mr. Savarini? He's in Switzerland; you can get his address from the books. I'm the only man he can trust—ask him, ask anyone. But I can't get the staff we want, see, so I don't have any chance to take up references. Tonight I'm two waiters short, and don't know whether any of the others will drop out. They just stop coming, that's what they do; it's plain ruddy hell, especially with this new catering-wages act. Ought to tear it up. To keep a staff of thirty we have to take on four or five new ones every week. English, Irish, French, Itye, Dutch, German—it's a proper UN. We could get women easier, but our clients don't like women waitresses, not in a high-class joint like this. So I might pick a bad waiter, who knows?"

"We all take the risk," Roger said easily. He didn't quite know why, but he was anxious not to antagonize this man; the conciliatory note had been set with Sarkey and was running right through. "Mind if I look at the pay sheet?"

"Help yourself," the man said, and unlocked the safe, then took out a large book. "There it is. Only don't keep me up here too long; Louis can start things, but when it comes to the real job, I can't trust him. I can't trust anyone, if it comes to that. I know what Mr. Savarini means, now."

Roger was scanning the list of names in the paybook.

There was no O'Leary, but there was "William Mulcaster."

So part of O'Leary's statement had been true. He himself might have given a different name here.

There were letters from a man who signed himself Emile Savarini, papers which showed Savarini as the owner. Hick was on the payroll at a thousand pounds a year.

Roger could check on Savarini, but it would take time.

He wished his hand wasn't hurting so much, but kept it tucked away, handed the paybook back, and asked:

"What car do you run, Mr. Hick?"

"Jaguar," Hick said offhandedly, "but I use an old Austin to run around in—does instead of a van. Lots of the private houses I cater at don't like vans outside; gives the game away." He came very near to grinning. "Thing you've got to remember is this: I can't help what my staff gets up to. Why, there was one chap, I fired him pretty quick, who used to borrow the Austin whenever he felt like it. He'd been doing it for weeks to run his girl friend around in; saw him driving it round Piccadilly one day. Nerve? Some people have the nerve of Old Harry!"

"Yes, haven't they?" Roger said dryly, and glanced at his watch.

It was half-past five. Everything had happened in a little over twenty minutes.

Then he remembered Barbara Denny again.

10

Visitors to Brickett Street

The woman at Jefferson's was a little bit flustered on the telephone.

"I don't think Miss Denny's here, sir, I think she left with Mr. Philip, but I'll see, please hold on." She didn't wait for Roger to answer, but put her receiver down.

Hick said, "I've got to go down and keep an eye on Louis. You let me know when you're finished up here." He dropped a bunch of keys on the desk. "There're the keys. *I've* got nothing to hide."

Roger said, "Thanks. Just one more question, and I needn't worry you any more now. What time were you here until last night?"

"Three-ish," Hick said promptly. "Had a couple who wouldn't go home."

"Was all the staff here?"

"Blimey, no. Just a couple—kid named Mulcaster and a part-timer who comes in sometimes to earn a few bob. He's not on the payroll, though."

"What's his name?'

"O'Leary."

That was that, if Hick was telling the truth, and certainly it all came out glibly.

Hick nodded, and drooped off. He had to duck to avoid knocking his chef's tall hat off against the lintel. He didn't look round. Roger pulled the wages book toward him and turned the pages over, using his right hand, supporting the telephone with the palm of his left. The fingers throbbed no matter where he held his hand. There was a page for each week in the book, and it went back nearly eighteen months. There had been no Mulcaster then—in April of last year. He listened to the crackling on the telephone, and turned page after page.

He found the first entry; Mulcaster's name first appeared in September, so he had worked here just over a year. His starting salary had been three pounds five shillings; today, it was five guineas. There was no entry for tips. A few of the salaries were high; most were on the low side. Hick hadn't lied about the number of transient workers needed to keep a regular staff of thirty. The list of names might have come from a modern Tower of Babel; they ranged from Witelosorsoki to Lin Yen. Each page had names which appeared only once in the book.

Hick didn't appear to have lied about Dillon, either; the dead man's name was entered at the foot of the page covering the previous week.

Dillon, S. J.   4 days   £2 12s. 6d.
   Waiter

"Are you there?" Jefferson's girl said at last.

"Yes."

"I'm awfully sorry to keep you, but Miss Denny *has* gone. She left about a quarter of an hour ago with Mr. Philip."

"With whom?"

"Why, Mr. Philip—Mr. Philip Sarkey."

"Oh," said Roger, and because she sounded surprised that he didn't seem to know, added, "Of course, sorry. Did she say where she was going?"

"No, sir, not as far as I can find out."

"All right, thanks," Roger said.

He rang off. Somewhere below him an electric machine was working steadily. Outside, everything was going on as usual, and probably the crowd had cleared away from Green Street, the damaged car would have been towed away, and in place of Dillon, S.J., there would be a patch of sawdust. People would step on it without wondering why it was there, cars would be driven over it, errand boys on bicycles would whistle as they cycled over. And a young man would probably be haunted by that crunching thud for the rest of his days.

Roger shook his head. He wouldn't be; people were tougher than that.

What was the matter with him? He ought to have his fingers bathed and dressed, he ought to search thoroughly here, taking advantage of Hick's offer, he ought to see Turnbull, he ought to find out more about O'Leary, Mulcaster, those peculiar things that had happened to Sarkey.

There was a tap at the door.

"Come in."

"Oh, you alone?" Turnbull opened the door with unusual stealth and stepped in. "Didn't think Hick'd leave a cop up here alone. There's a man I wouldn't trust with my wallet or my wife. Found any hint?"

"No."

"Same here. Nothing in the veg bins, wine bins or garbage bins, except a few old sacks and a few new ones. The make we know all about. The head kitchen boy they call him, says they use a new sack every time they go to an outside job, to carry vegetables and the rougher stuff Plausible. And Dillon didn't come on the payroll until last week. I can't wait to see what was found in Dillon's pockets."

"No," said Roger, stonily. "Look, I've got to have this hand seen to, and I've a couple of rush jobs, too. Go through this office, will you? Account books, records, everything. Never mind what Hick says; if you have to stay here all night, stay all night."

"Okay." Turnbull stared at the bruised fingers. "That's nasty; you get it fixed."

"Thanks," said Roger. "Listen. Keep Hick sweet if you can. It was his Austin and we could have a go at him, but don't be too hard. He could be up to his neck in this, or just a stooge."

"Okay," Turnbull said.

"Did you ask him where he parked the Austin last night?"

"He says it was in a side street—he moved it this morning." Roger grunted.

He didn't go to the Yard at once, but before reaching his car, went into a chemist's and had his hand bathed. A fuzzy-haired pharmacist in a white jacket told him that he ought to have it properly dressed, and certainly shouldn't use it for a few days. He compromised by having the two middle fingers bandaged, as both were badly grazed and bruised, then went to his car. The police had moved it into a vacant space by the curb.

Until you hurt a hand, you didn't realize how often you used it.

It was six o'clock.

This was a good time to go and see Mulcaster, who had had a thousand opportunities to pump Jem Maitland about the watchmen's patrol schedule at Jefferson's. He must go very carefully with Mulcaster. The youth hadn't the personality to be the leader of the Gelignite Gang, but there was an ugly streak in him. It might pay big dividends to break his nerve gradually. Certainly it would be a mistake to get tough yet.

Roger wondered if Barbara Denny had gone to see Rosie.

Driving wasn't comfortable with his damaged hand, and traffic was thick with the evening rush hour. He had to concentrate, but thoughts edged their way into his mind. It was always the same; a case dragged on, there was blind alley after blind alley, and one's mind became fogged. Then too much happened at once. Rosie's film-star image of a husband, and Rosie herself, would have been enough in themselves for a day or two. Then O'Leary. Then Hick and the restaurant. Then Dillon. So there was too much to do, and he had to delegate some of it or get around to it too late.

At least he wasn't going to Brickett Street simply to chaperone Barbara Denny.

He found himself smiling wryly.

Two uniformed policemen and a crowd of all shapes and sizes at the corner of Brickett Street worried Roger. He went along too quickly, then had to swerve when a dog jumped into the road, put too much pressure on his left fingers, and bumped into the curb. A policeman looked up with annoyance, didn't recognize him, came forward and demanded:

"What do you think you're doing?"

"Sorry. What's up?"

"Who do you think—" The constable, peering in at the window, recognized Roger; his head bobbed out of sight with his start of surprise. He opened the door quickly. "Sorry, sir. Nothing much is up, don't often get a Rolls-Bentley in Brickett Street, that's all."

"A *what?*"

"Seven thousand pounds' worth of Rolls-Bentley, all the best of British workmanship!" The constable was talking too quickly, trying to regain his poise. "Hurt your hand, sir?"

"That's the trouble; I'm not drunk!" Roger smiled and turned toward Number 28.

There was the Bentley Continental, just about the most expensive car in the world. It was black, sleek, and gleaming, a dream on four wheels. It even impressed Roger as he moved toward its dark opulence. Several dozen children were crowding in about it, peering into the luxurious interior, breathing on the shining coachwork, grimacing at their reflection in the silver plating, dodging a policeman who was on guard.

"She can't be right in the head," Roger muttered. He strode to the door, nodding to the policeman who was keeping the kids off the car. He rapped sharply at the door and heard voices in the pause that followed. Then Mulcaster opened the door.

He had shaved, dressed, and pomaded his long, wavy black hair. He wore a collar and tie and a well-cut, pale blue suit. He was a tall, absurdly handsome youth who ought to have been boxed up and sent to Hollywood; the only weakness was at his mouth, and, perhaps, his chin. He looked bewildered, and didn't recognize Roger at once.

"What—what is it?"

"Is your wife in?" Roger asked. "I'd like a word with her."

"Who is it?" Mulcaster peered more closely, and then recognition came. He moved back sharply, catching his breath.

"Billy, tell them to go away," Rosie called. She sounded very tired. "I can't stand any more visitors just now, I really can't. I—I'm ever so sorry, Miss Barbara," she went on after a brief pause, "but I've got an awful headache. I don't mean to be rude. Not to *you*."

"We should never have come," a man said in a deep voice—one which Cortland called sardonically the Upper Ten voice, a kind of Oxford plus. "Come along, Barbara."

"Wait for me outside, Philip, please."

"No, I'm damned if I will!"

108

Roger pushed past Billy Mulcaster, who still seemed more puzzled than scared.

The little room seemed crowded.

Rosie stood with her back to the fireplace. She'd taken her hair out of curlers; it was nice, fair hair, but not her crowning glory. She had powdered her face and touched her lips with lipstick, and in the gloom of the room she was quite startlingly beautiful. Her eyes were very bright—too bright; she certainly had a headache. Roger was much more vividly aware of her figure than he had been that morning, perhaps because she was wearing a flowered cotton dress which was too tight.

Barbara Denny said, "It's perfectly all right, Rosie, I'll come again when you're feeling better. Please believe that I only want to help you."

"Oh, I *do!*"

The taller woman turned away.

She had that curious gift of changing her expression in a flash. Her look at Rosie had been one of understanding mingled with distress; her look at the man by her side was one of sharp annoyance, perhaps disdain. Then she saw who had arrived, and was taken completely by surprise, just looked at Roger blankly.

So did the man, Philip Sarkey.

He was shorter than Barbara, but very broad-shouldered, with a young lion of a head and a lion's mane of coarse, fair hair. Roger knew all about him, now. Until a year or so ago his big features and rugged masculinity had been familiar to millions. Phil Sarkey, as a motor-racing ace, had a big following. A glance was enough to tell of great physical strength and to hint at reckless courage. Roger knew that he was twenty-five; he looked nearer thirty-five. Barbara Denny, who was in the late thirties, might have claimed twenty-six or -seven and fooled a lot of people.

"Sorry I'm late," Roger said. "but perhaps you understand better why I offered to escort you." He saw disdain dawning on Barbara Denny's face because he had failed to keep his word; then his mind began to work properly. He was fully aware of Billy Mulcaster's half-scared, half-cunning expression, as he smiled slightly at Barbara Denny. "There was some trouble in Soho, nasty business —shooting and a death."

Barbara said, "Oh, I'm sorry!" All hint of disdain disappeared.

"Anything to do with this business?" Philip Sarkey demanded sharply.

"It could be," Roger said. "It started at a little restaurant, a place called the Pretzel." He was pretending to look at Sarkey, but was actually intent on Billy Mulcaster's face.

11

Interview

Billy didn't even look shocked, and that was a mistake. It proved that he had schooled himself to show no expression.

"I know the place," Philip Sarkey said carelessly. "Still, it hardly affects us."

Rosie was looking at Billy as if she couldn't understand why he didn't announce that he worked at Pretzel's. Something in her husband's expression kept her silent. It wasn't a nice look; certainly not a lover's.

Mulcaster wanted watching closely.

He was gripping the door frame. It seemed as if, at times of mental stress, he needed physical support. He had his mouth closed tightly, and his eyes narrowed at Roger. There was something about Roger's gaze that he didn't like. He turned away. His beautifully shaped hand slid down the door frame with a stealthy kind of movement.

"We were at Pretzel's only a few nights ago," Barbara Denny said. "We often—" She broke off.

"It's the best place for food in London," Philip

Sarkey declared. "I hope you aren't going to close it down!" The flippancy was only partly forced. He took Barbara's arm. "Darling, I'm sorry I've been sour, you're probably much more right than I am. Come here again when things have quieted down a bit, or better still, have—er—Rosie come and see you." He smiled at Rosie and at Barbara; suddenly it was he, not Billy Mulcaster, who might have stepped straight off a film set.

"We won't close it down," Roger said. He was backing toward the door to see what Mulcaster was up to. There were no footsteps on the stairs, so the youth had gone into the kitchen; and there was a back way out. "Mr. Sarkey, if you want any car left I'd go and look after it; there's a swarm of kids arguing whether it is a car or a flying saucer." He opened the door in time to see an exasperated policeman clip a ten-year-old boy on the side of the head. The boy jumped off the Rolls-Bentley and put his tongue out, but didn't hit back. "Officer," Roger breathed into the man's ear, making him spring to attention. "Go round the back. If Mulcaster—know him?"

"Yes, *sir*."

"Just stop him. Tell the others at the end of the road but don't let the crowd hear."

"Right, sir, but the car—"

"The kids won't hurt the car."

Roger moved swiftly back to the front door. Barbara was coming out, and he stood aside for her. "Sorry again," he said briskly, "but it would be better if you left now. I'll keep in touch."

He went back into the little front room.

Philip Sarkey, moving toward the door, was glancing round at Rosie. She was really something

112

to look at; hers was the kind of body that could torment a man.

"See you later, Sarkey," Roger said briefly. "I won't be long, Mrs. Mulcaster." He heard a door open at the back; a draft cut in, stirring a newspaper. "Is O'Leary here?"

"Who—who?"

"The man who was here this morning."

"No," she said drearily, "he doesn't live here."

Roger smiled, said, "Why don't you sit down?" and moved in and across the kitchen like a flash. The door was wide open and led into a small, cemented yard. He stepped into this. Mulcaster was at a narrow gate in the wall, almost touching a dustbin as he leaned across to open it. He was looking round, and, when he saw Roger, hostility shone in his eyes.

He didn't move.

"Why didn't you say you worked at Pretzel's?" Roger asked sharply.

The pale, handsome face was set.

"Didn't you know?"

"I know a lot of things. Where were you at two o'clock this morning?"

"Pretzel's."

"You're lying."

Mulcaster sneered. "Think so?"

It was like a brick wall—or a steel wall.

"How well do you know Dillon?" Roger asked abruptly.

"Dillon?" echoed Mulcaster. Then his glance flashed up, past Roger's head, toward the upper-floor window of the house. Something had caught his eye. It didn't rest there long, but when he looked away he seemed to sneer. Otherwise, his face was quite expressionless. "What about Dillon?" His voice was suddenly louder.

Was there someone up in the top room?

Roger didn't turn round, didn't show that he had noticed anything, but he felt a cold, clammy hand at the back of his neck, and the coldness crept up and down his spine. He knew what it was: just old-fashioned fear. This was a killer's game; if Dillon hadn't killed the night watchman, then a killer might be up in that room.

Roger remembered the policeman in Ash Street falling back from a bullet wound, and Dillon shooting at him.

"Let's get back into the house," Roger said. He put a hand on Mulcaster's arm, then turned round and caught a glimpse of a shadowy figure before a man darted behind a curtain. O'Leary? Roger pretended not to have noticed; only his glance flickered upward, his head didn't lift as he went on calmly, "How long have you known him?"

"Who?"

"Dillon."

"Only—only a few days."

"How did you meet?"

"He came—he came to work at Pretzel's," Billy Mulcaster said. They entered the dark kitchen, and Mulcaster's defiance was sullen and tough. "What are you asking all these questions for?"

Roger said, "Dillon was killed in an accident this afternoon. He had a gun. We want to know all we can about him. Did he have any special friends at Pretzel's?"

"If he did, it wasn't me," Billy sneered. He moved swiftly toward the front room and stepped to Rosie's side, as if her presence gave him strength, her body gave support. His voice became shrill. Now he blustered. "I'd never seen Dillon before, hardly knew him, why, I didn't even like him! It isn't right, worrying me and my wife like this, after what happened, isn't that bad enough? There are plenty of other people you can ask—why don't you? Why come and worry us? And keep that pair of nosy Parkers out of here, see! I don't want them here any more. Understand?"

Roger made himself say, "I can't stop them from coming. I advised Miss Denny not to. She only wants to help."

"We don't want her help. We do all right."

"Don't make too many mistakes," Roger said roughly.

Now he paid more attention to Rosie. She looked desperately ill, her big eyes were glassy, and obviously her husband's manner bewildered her. Frightened her? Her voice held desperation.

"Oh, please don't talk any more," she pleaded, "I've got an awful headache, I have really."

"Why don't you get out of here?" Mulcaster muttered.

"I'll want to see you again," Roger said. He wanted to get under Mulcaster's skin and yet to ease the girl's burden.

She didn't speak again.

Roger went to the door. He heard a faint sound above his head, but didn't look up; Rosie did, agitatedly.

"Was Dillon on duty last night?" Roger asked abruptly.

"You know damned well he was if you've been to Pretzel's," Mulcaster said.

"Did you see him there all the time? Was he out

between—" Roger hesitated, with the door open and in his hand, while Mulcaster held Rosie's shoulder much as he used door frames—"two o'clock and three?"

"Couldn't have—he left before one."

"Sure?"

"I ought to know, oughtn't I? I was on late turn."

"How many others were late?"

"The chef, Hick, and my pal O'Leary."

"No more?"

"I didn't look under the tables," Mulcaster sneered.

Rosie just closed her eyes.

"All right," Roger said. "But it had better be true."

He went out, closing the door quietly, and as he closed it, glanced round at Rosie. She was free from Billy's hold now, and staring up into his strikingly handsome face, her own profile startlingly lovely.

"Oh, Billy," she whispered, "what is it, what have you done?"

"Don't you worry," Mulcaster said. "They've got nothing on me."

Roger closed the door.

Rosie looked up into her young husband's face and felt sure that he was lying. His eyes were hot and angry, his hands gripped her shoulders painfully. Most of the afternoon he had been as kind and affectionate as a man could be, helping her to get through the awful hours; he had even made her smile once or twice. But she had known that he was worried, and that had shown more vividly when O'Leary had come again.

She could remember him coming in, now; he had let himself in with a key. She didn't realize the significance of that until afterward.

He'd said, "Just want a word with you, Billy boy."

That had been about five o'clock.

Billy and Rosie had been in the kitchen, sitting over a cup of tea at the big table, when O'Leary had arrived. The two men had gone into the front room. Rosie had heard them talking in low-pitched whispers, and now and again Billy had said, "Okay, okay," or "You can trust me." Then he had gone out, telling her that he was going to get the *Evening News*, to see how Clip-Clip had got on in the 3:30 at Newmarket.

After he had gone, O'Leary had come in, moving very quietly; he seldom seemed to make a sound. He'd just grinned at her, putting that funny-shaped head on one side, and she had felt a new, a different kind of fear, a desire to scream because of things she did not understand, because of the things which this man seemed to hint at, without saying a word.

Then:

"Billy's a good boy, Rosie, I like him a lot, and I've been a good pal of his, see. Why, if it wasn't for me, Billy wouldn't have half the luck he gets. The tips I give him! And now he's doing me a service, Rosie." O'Leary had come near and slid his arm round her waist, squeezing her tightly, unbearably familiar. His big hands! She had held her breath to stop herself from screaming at him. Thank heavens, he hadn't stayed like that long. "And so can you, Rosie. Just think of Billy boy, will you, and remember how much I can influence his future. Don't tell anyone I'm here, see. Not a soul."

She'd swung away from him as soon as his arm had dropped.

"Who—who's after you?"

"Oh, no one's after me," O'Leary had said, "not even the flippin' narks, but I just don't want anyone to know I'm here. Get it? Billy wouldn't want you to tell anyone, and I could do Billy a lot of harm."

"What do you mean?"

He had just stood there, grinning.

When Billy had come back, he hadn't brought the *Evening News*. He hadn't looked so good, either. In a rough voice he had ordered Rosie not to tell anyone that O'Leary was here.

Then the next two visitors had called—Miss Barbara, whom Rosie knew quite well, but who was from a different world, and the powerful, ugly man with the big head, who had looked at her—Rosie—as so many men did, and had done from her early teens. Nakedly.

Next the policeman had come from Scotland Yard.

Now Billy was lying. Underneath his hardness, she believed that he was badly frightened. Who but O'Leary was a cause of his fear? She didn't understand. She didn't think she wanted to understand, because whenever she started to think about it, she realized that the change in Billy had really been born when Inspector West had come that morning; it had started with the news of the murder of her father.

Hers were nameless, hideous fears.

"Listen, I haven't done a thing," Billy insisted.

"It's this man Dillon whom West is worrying about. *I* can't help it if a crook gets a job in my place, can I? Don't look at me like that!" He swung away from her. "I've got to go to work, can't stay here all night!"

He was at the door, hand against the frame.

She was horrified.

"But Billy, you said Mr. Hick had given you some time off!"

"I just phoned him, I've got to go in, he's short on waiters tonight—and what the hell, I don't have to tell you everything, do I? I don't have to ask your permission to go to *work!*"

He flung himself up the stairs.

Rosie sat on the edge of a chair and stared at the window, the faint light of a gaslamp outside, the shadowy street, the yellow oblong of a window across the road. Her eyes were dry. She felt empty, hopeless, despairing, as if she had lost more than her father.

Upstairs, O'Leary was at the bedroom door to greet Billy. Billy pushed past him.

"Listen, Billy, you get too excited," O'Leary said. "Keep calm, boy. Don't say a word more to West or any copper, just tie a knot in your tongue when they're around, see. They'll be satisfied with Dillon, they won't reach you or me. Just keep your mouth shut and everything will be all right. And don't answer back. Nasty things could happen to you, Billy. Nasty things could happen to little wifey, too. Just you tie that knot."

12

Facts Thick and Fast

Roger West spoke into the telephone while looking up at Turnbull, who was standing and grinning across the desk in the office at the Yard.

"I'm sorry, darling, I just can't make it, but I don't think I'll be very late....Say good night to the boys for me, and make do with television instead of the pictures....Yes, of course I'm all right....Listen, sweet, I'd love to hear about it, but I'm in one hell of a rush."

There was a longer pause.

Then he laughed. "All right, I'll remember to take care of myself!"He rang off, pushed the telephone away from him, then poked his fingers through his hair. "Take that grin off your face, Warren, and sit down. Did you order those sandwiches?"

"They're on the way." Turnbull sat on an upright chair, aggressively good-looking but in a very different way from Billy Mulcaster. "I ordered some beer, too. How's your hand?"

"All right." Since Roger had arrived at the Yard,

the hand had been properly dressed. It was now more nuisance than anxiety. "Well, what did you get?"

"Beggar all."

"Absolute blank?"

"Absolute is the word," Turnbull said. "The records are all there, going back two years, to the time when Savarini bought the place. Savarini's got a spot on his chest, and is in Switzerland. Hick manages the joint. Pay sheets, invoices, receipts, everything on the up-and-up, as far as I can see. And what a business! Know how much it turns over in a week?"

"How much?"

"One thousand five hundred quid, and a helluva big margin of profit. The money's mostly banked in Savarini's name—Hick only draws on a working account."

Roger said, "So he's honest, on top." He looked through some papers quickly. "We've tackled four waiters who left at one o'clock last night. Dillon hadn't left by then. Four members of the staff and a couple of late diners were there. Short of asking help from the press or the B.B.C. we can't find those diners. So the four on the staff could have been at Jefferson's, not Pretzel's."

"What beats me is the fact that they used Hick's Austin," Turnbull said.

"We'd have a job to break his explanation," Roger reflected. "But they can get overconfident, though, like O'Leary. O'Leary was at the Mulcasters', lying low," he added. "Be interesting to see where he goes next."

"Can the Division cope at the place?"

Roger grinned. "Better ask Sopley!"

A policeman in uniform brought in some white-bread sandwiches, with fat ham overlapping the crusts, and two pint bottles of light ale.

"Fine!" Roger bit into a sandwich, and Turnbull opened a bottle and poured ale into battered pewter tankards.

"Sure about Hick's dishonesty?" Roger asked suddenly.

"Damned right I'm sure. I can smell it!"

Another sergeant might have got a sharp rebuke for guessing. Turnbull didn't. These two worked together a great deal, and Turnbull could handle routine with thrice the speed of the average sergeant; he wasn't often slapdash, either. As men, they didn't really like each other, and probably never would, but they had the job to do. So Roger was forbearing, and Turnbull usually sensed when he was on the verge of going too far and called a halt.

He didn't now.

"I think I've checked everything you asked me to. First, Dillon. He's a bachelor, been inside for breaking and entering. He's been a traveling salesman for the past six months—guess what kind of tradesmen he called on?"

Roger said, "Jewelers."

"We must have telepathic minds! He had quite a big connection by offering so-called bankrupt stocks at cutthroat discounts. We're digging hard for his source of supply but haven't been able to find anything yet. Girls in every town he travels, judging from the stack of love letters at his flat in Victoria. He won't be sullying *their* virtue again." Turnbull was speaking now in a level but harsh voice. "He usually traveled alone in a small van, and we haven't found the van. I've asked all London and Home County Divisions to keep an eye open for it. Got the number and description in the log book, which I found at his flat."

"We'd better make a note to start questioning the girl friends if we don't soon get all we need." Roger scribbled on a pad.

"Sometimes Dillon drove a big American car, too," Turnbull went on. "A Packard. Coincidence, eh? That's about everything on Dillon. No known association with Mulcaster or O'Leary except through the restaurant, and O'Leary isn't on the staff there, just does jobs for them."

"Next?" said Roger.

"I'd hate the day you ever stepped into Chatworth's shoes; we call *him* a slave driver." But Turnbull grinned. "Mulcaster flashes the corn about plenty. He seems to win on everything from the pools downwards. Remarkable, isn't it?"

"Very. Since when?"

"Past nine months or so—since just after the G.G. boys started. Before that he decorated all the dance halls in the East End and a few in the West End; he was the beau of all the belles. Then he and Rosie Maitland met. Can't get a whisper from anyone against Rosie or her father," Turnbull went on, "and it seems to have been love at first sight. After he met her, Billy didn't look at another pair of bloomers. I'm told the poppet's quite a dream."

"You'd agree," Roger said.

"I must get assigned to that end of the job." Turnbull gave an almost wolfish grin. "There's nothing on O'Leary anywhere. I telephoned AZ, and gave them the description you'd given me, and they're checking. Keeping it dark, as you said.

123

Then there's the old Austin. We haven't touched it, apart from the ten minutes looking in the back and finding those bits of hessian and the sparkler. No reason why Hick or anyone else should have been warned because we got onto it, is there?"

"Let's remember that it doesn't have to be Hick," Roger cautioned.

"Ten to one on, but have it your own way."

"Tell me why a man obviously in line for a partnership in a business showing a big gross profit would throw everything up for a risk like the Gelignite Gang boys take," Roger argued.

Turnbull was a long time answering. Then:

"If a man's born bad, he's bad," he said flatly. "That restaurant's a wonderful cover. Strangers come and go, no one asks why. Take it from me, we haven't seen so much light since the G.G. boys began."

"We want facts, not light," Roger said dryly. He was thinking of young Martin and his question, and his own part answer about men who were born bad. "Anything else?"

"I thought you'd like to know the kind of clientele that they have at the Pretzel Restaurant," Turnbull said, and the fact that he kept a poker face told Roger that this was the sting he had kept for the tail. He handed over two typewritten sheets, each filled with two columns of names— about a hundred and fifty names in all. "Belted earls and bloated aristocracy, prelates, and parsons, press barons and financial magicians, maestros of business, the stage, the screen, television, and radio—what a gilt-edged list!" Turnbull bellowed that, unable to keep a poker face any longer. "Just look at it, Handsome! They all run accounts.

There's more money in that little lot than in the rest of London put together."

Roger was reading. "Yes, it's quite a list. You forgot to mention the politicians and the diplomats. How does a place get a reputation like that?"

"Good cooking," said Turnbull. "The Sarkeys go there too, both Sir Gerald and Philip. By the way, you've met Barbara Denny. Did you know that she and Philip Sarkey are engaged? They—hell, what's happening to my mind, I knew I'd forgotten something! You asked AZ to check jewelers to see if any local ones had sold Mulcaster an engagement ring for his sweetie. The answer is no. Prize ring, was it?"

"Seven hundred pounds' worth of diamond or else a few shillings' worth of paste or rhinestone," Roger said. Then he remembered that he hadn't noticed it on Rosie's finger on his second visit. He must check. "Sure about this engagement between Philip Sarkey and Barbara Denny? I don't remember reading about it, and it would hit the press in a big way."

"I got it from Caroline Wellesley, Sir Gerald's piece of efficiency. She isn't the old maid she looks." Turnbull grinned. "You know she told us about her boss's secret troubles. Well, I told her how grateful we were, etc., etc., and did she know anyone who might wish the old boy ill?" Turnbull chuckled. "First thing she said, Sir G. isn't so old, only just sixty. She's right, too, and fit as many a man of fifty, I'd say. Then she said no—she'd never met anyone with a grudge against the Cold Fish. There'd been a bit of feeling lately, because Philip was so keen on Barbara. Sir Gerald was known to disapprove because Barbara is ten years or more older than Philip. Between you and me," Turnbull went on, "Sir Gerald's disapproval of Barbara's interest in Rosie Mulcaster might spring from displeasure at Barbara's baby snatching."

"Baby snatching's the word," Roger said dryly, and pictured Philip Sarkey's lion's head.

"Actually, if Caroline Wellesley knows what she's talking about, Philip's done all the attacking and Barbara's only just given way," Turnbull went on. "They're keeping it from papa and the press." Turnbull gave a broad grin. "Anything new turned up with you?"

Roger ignored the implied, "Have *you* done anything?"

"Not really," he said. "O'Leary isn't being tagged, but every copper in London now has his description, and we're digging deep. I don't think we can do anything else except look for that Packard. We could really go to town on that."

"I don't get you," Turnbull said.

"I'm going to ask Chatworth to okay a check on every prewar Packard known to be in London. One of those nice, quiet jobs the Divisions like so much. You don't seem to notice many Packards, but they're about in the hundreds. If we can connect one with Dillon or Hick, Mulcaster or O'Leary, we might really be on the move." Roger was crisp, definite. "Then I want the Divisions combed for a man who can get a job as a waiter or kitchen hand at Pretzel's. A French or Italian type, preferably one with some restaurant experience. He mustn't come from Central or AZ, because he might be recognized. Will you—"

"I know just the one. Chap named Marino, out at Hammersmith," Turnbull said.

"Fine." Roger nodded.

The telephone bell rang. He glanced at a big clock with black hands, on the wall above the fireplace, and grimaced. It was nearly half-past eight.

"Don't say anything else has started.... West, here ... Who?" He sounded startled. "Oh, yes, put him through ..." He put the mouthpiece against his chest and said to Turnbull, "Philip Sarkey. There's a turn up for the book."

They paused.

Young Sarkey said, "Chief Inspector West?"

"Speaking."

"I'm sorry to add to your burdens," young Sarkey said, "but can you spare me half an hour? I think there's a way in which I can help you and I know there's a way you can help me. I don't think you'll feel that the time has been wasted."

This was humility with a vengeance. Like father, unlike son—but Philip had been the son of his arrogant father at Brickett Street.

"I'll be glad to try," Roger said. "When and where?"

"As soon as you can, and in the next hour or so preferably. Perhaps you'd care to come to my flat. I could send a car—"

"No, thanks. I won't have a lot of time, but I could come almost straight away," Roger said. "What address?"

"Number 5 Parable Court—that's not far from Park Lane near the Dorchester."

"I know it," Roger said.

"You're very good."

"Not at all. Good-by."

Roger rang off and sat back, forming a little O

127

with his lips. Turnbull grinned. The silence lasted for some minutes before Roger said:

"Fix that waiter, and then there's one other thing to work on. Your friend Hick. You say he started to manage Pretzel's a year ago. What did he do for a living before that? Busy tonight?"

"Always on duty, that's me," said Turnbull.

13

Message

Earlier that evening, when Philip Sarkey had driven Barbara Denny away from Brickett Street, there had been a marked constraint between them. Now and again Sarkey glanced at the woman, but she stared steadily in front of her. They were driving along the Embankment, approaching Westminster Bridge, when Sarkey said abruptly:

"That's where your friend West spends his time." He took a hand off the wheel and pointed to a big gray building behind a high gray wall.

Barbara said, "Surely Scotland Yard's built of red brick."

"Part of it is. The traffic cops and the civil side of it are in red buildings. The new building houses the C.I.D." Sarkey seemed to relax. "Barbara, I am all kinds of a swine, and I'm desperately sorry."

She looked at him, her eyes shadowed. "Oh, Phil, if only you knew how I want to help. If—" She broke off.

"I think I do now," said Philip Sarkey. "I didn't, out there. But—oh, I don't know. I don't like being frozen out by my wife-to-be, and—oh, why the hell can't I handle words!" He drove past the Houses of Parliament and then slowed up, stopping by the curb side on the Embankment. "I can't talk and drive, never could! Barbara, I hate the thought of you going to hovels like that but I think I'm beginning to see what drives you. That girl tonight looked—well, she looked as if she was starving for help. But face it, sweetheart; do you think you really did help her?"

Barbara looked away from him.

He took her hand. "Do you?"

"No," she said, in a taut voice. "No, I didn't then. But later, I think I can."

"I don't know," Philip said. "But I do know this, and it has to be said. The Old Man will cut up really rough if you keep this up. He didn't say much today, he was rather taken by that chap West, but I saw him this afternoon. He was quite emphatic. Either you drop the—well, 'slumming's' the word he used; it's brutal but I can't think of another—or he'll put the bar up."

In the same taut voice, Barbara said, "What does that mean?"

"It means that he'll keep you out of Jefferson's," said Philip, and his fingers tightened on her hand. "It means he'll cut you off, and we know he's capable of it. He did it to Reggie, his own son—and that would mean I'd have to leave him and come with you. You know I would like a shot, but do we want a family schism, darling? You'd be sorry. He'll come round to you and me, eventually, but if you keep needling him—well, he might not be so ready to give thousands of pounds away to charities run by his titled friends."

Barbara said very quietly, "That's a mean thing to say, Philip. He does it because he thinks it's right."

Philip suddenly squeezed her hands tightly.

"You really believe that, don't you? Know the trouble with you, Bar? You're too good. You look only for good in others—and that's just as well when I'm around! But Dad isn't a natural do-gooder. I think he gives away his thousands for two reasons—(a) you make out a wonderful case for the charities, (b) he's always being stung by his conscience. He wishes he hadn't cut Reginald right off, and this is his form of atonement. But if you and I deliberately defy him—well, we'll run into trouble. We don't want to be treated as Reggie was."

After a long pause, Barbara said quietly:

"I think you're wrong about his motives, Phil, but that's beside the point. I don't want there to be any misunderstandings. I shall go on doing what I think I ought to do. If Gerald wants to cut me off, I should be sorry but I'd accept it. I can earn my own living, you know; I don't have to have his help and we are not related. I could find more than enough to do. And if that happened, you and I would have to break things off. You could no more live in comparative poverty than I could live forever in a palace." She glanced at the dashboard clock; it was nearly six thirty. "You must hurry; you're having a drink with two of the board tonight, aren't you?"

Philip said, "Yes, at seven, confound it. Look here, Bar, I've made a hash of this; I always do. But listen. I think you're wrong about one thing. I *could* live wherever you lived, in plenty or penury."

She looked at him steadily.

"Could you?" she asked.

And he didn't answer.

He left her, twenty minutes later, at the small flat in a small house near Berkeley Square. She gave him rather a brittle smile, and didn't wave from the door.

Barbara went into her bedroom, took off her hat, ran a comb through her lovely chestnut hair, and looked at her reflection. She felt inwardly cold, almost frozen. She believed that a clash between Philip and his father would be a terrible one. She knew only a garbled version of the old family scandal. It was a miserable situation, and she disliked the secrecy. But Gerald Sarkey seemed to compel others to act without his knowledge.

In a way, Philip was frightened of his father, and very, very anxious not to upset him. She had never been sure of the wisdom of promising to marry Philip; she was quite sure, now, that he wasn't the right man for her.

She must break it off. Soon.

The decision helped a little.

She looked brighter when she went into the small dining alcove. She chatted with her maid for a few minutes, enjoyed a casserole of chicken, a cream caramel, and coffee, and was settling down to embroidering, a magazine, and her thoughts when the telephone bell rang.

Philip?

He would be with the other directors.

"Hello? This is Barbara Denny."

A man said hurriedly, "Sorry to worry yer, Miss Denny, but I gotta messich for yer. From Rosie Mulcaster, Brickett Street, you know. Rosie says

132

can you come to see 'er? Needs 'elp proper bad, she does. Could you come strite away?"

"Oh, of course," Barbara said, and her eyes lit up. "Of course! Tell her I'll be there within an hour."

"She was sure you wouldn't let her dahn," the man said, and rang off.

Leary stepped out of a telephone booth at a corner near Brickett Street, looked across at the lighted windows of the Red Bull public house, thrust both hands into his raincoat pockets, and then grinned at his companion.

"Hook, line, and sinker," he said. "She could have kissed me, she was so pleased. So we can move along nicely, and it'll all work out. She'll come as fast as she knows how, too—I wonder what she'd say if she knew what she was coming into."

He laughed softly in the quiet, misty night.

There were three worlds. The world of Brickett Street and the East End's seamier districts; the world of Bell Street, Chelsea, and Roger West's pleasant stratum of lower-middle-income group, and the world of Rolls-Bentleys and luxury Mayfair flats. Each was quite distinct from the other two. Stepping into the apartments at Parable Court, Roger knew exactly what he was doing. The world of Rolls-Bentleys was not unfamiliar to him, for crime took him into unlikely places and bowed the most improbable heads.

It was a small block of flats, two to each of the five floors. A uniformed commissionaire took Roger to the second floor, and delivered him into the hands of a footman dressed in black and with a long pale face which looked too unreal ever to relax. He asked Roger to wait in an opulent armchair in an opulent hall, and went off, silent as a dark ghost.

Round these walls were little gems—by Corot, Matisse, and names less illustrious but highly regarded from the Seine to the Hudson River. There was subdued wall lighting, a hush, as if this were a kind of sanctuary, a holy place. A house of worship for the god of money?

The butler appeared, still wraithlike and sonorous.

"If you will please come this way, sir."

Roger got up, started after him, and was surprised when Philip Sarkey came hurrying from a room at the far end of a narrow passage. Philip was in a dinner jacket, beautifully cut, sitting proudly on his magnificent shoulders. It was impossible to ignore his ugliness, as impossible not to be affected by his smile of welcome—not one of full power, like at Brickett Street, but impressive none the less.

He held out his hand.

"Very good of you to come so promptly. Do come in." The Oxford-plus voice was not so irritating in these surroundings. They went into a small room, book-lined, with comfortable leather armchairs, a thick carpet, an open fire as well as central heating. Brandy glowed in a glass and in a decanter on a small, low table by the fire, which reflected on the rounded glass. A small trolley held bottles of whisky, rum, gin, three different vermouths, soda, squashes, and two bottles of beer. "What can I get you?" Philip asked when Roger was sitting down.

"I think I'll stick to beer."

"Sure? Well, all right." Philip unstoppered a bottle. Roger leaned back in the easy chair, bandaged hand on one arm. There were cigarettes at hand; Philip was determined to do him well, was extremely anxious to be friendly. He must want something he was almost sure that he wouldn't get, Roger thought. The man's hand was steady—a big hand, not ugly like O'Leary's but very different from the slender one of his father—as he poured out pale beer.

He moved, and stood with his back to the fire, brandy glass cupped in his hands, leonine head raised as he looked at a picture on the far wall, as if he were consulting it for guidance. Then he turned to Roger. He had shaggy, gold-colored eyebrows, and his rugged face seemed more than ever like a lion's.

"I'm speaking in confidence, of course; it is a personal matter, and yet it may also affect your investigation. It's about my fian—about Miss Denny. I'm very worried about her. For years she has taken an interest in the welfare work at the store, and of course no one has discouraged her. Forgive me if I put it this way—having an income of her own, she has always felt that she ought to contribute something to the people less fortunate than she is, and her conscience has always been very quick to react. As a result, she has mixed with some odd people. Her visit to Brickett Street this evening, for instance, is in character. I confess I handled it badly, I've no finesse—you should hear my father call me a bull in a china shop!—I don't think I discouraged Barbara at all. In fact she will probably be more determined than ever to go and

135

try to help this girl—ah—Rosie. I'd much rather she didn't. As I made clear at the beginning, this isn't your affair as a Yard man, or as an individual for that matter, but if you could discourage her from this—ah—slumming, I'd be extremely grateful. So would my father. It isn't that we don't approve of welfare schemes. All of our stores have excellent welfare arrangements—pension, sickness benefits, that kind of thing. But—well, this is a most unsavory business, isn't it? I don't know whether you can do anything at all, but if you do get a chance, will you?"

Philip stopped.

Roger could say "yes" and it wouldn't make any difference. If this were the real reason why the man had asked him to come, it suggested a high degree of desperation.

"You see," Philip went on hesitantly at first, "if it goes too far, I'm afraid that Barbara will make a kind of martyr of herself for this Mulcaster girl. It can become a kind of test case as to how far Barbara can go. I'm sorry to throw this at you, West, but I don't think my father will stand any more of it. He's always disliked it intensely when she has worked outside the store itself, and she does a lot of sick visiting, and that kind of thing. I'm afraid that if she ties herself up with Rosie—that *is* the girl's name, isn't it?—and this dago-looking husband of hers, she might find herself really in trouble." The words came more swiftly now. "You know—cut-off-with-a-shilling kind of nonsense. But my father is a martinet, and he'll stand so much and not a thing more. He made it pretty clear to me that it will mean a family estrangement if she gets involved. That happened once in the family, and—er—I don't want it to happen again. I'd stand by Barbara, of course, but it would be a hell of a break. Very proud man, my father. Er—he doesn't know I'm being so embarrassingly frank with you, of course, but Barbara has formed a pretty high opinion of you—apparently you handled Father with a touch of genius this morning! I think she would be guided by you. As a family matter it is of vital importance."

Philip sipped his brandy, then stepped nervously to a side table, selected a cigar from a box, remembered himself and brought the box across, held it out to Roger, and went on:

"Well, that's that! I won't make this situation even more difficult by asking you to say yea or nay now—if you'll think about it, and find you can help, I'll be eternally grateful. So will Barbara, although she won't realize the need for it. Do have one of these. I brought them back from Bermuda last winter; couldn't hope to find a better cigar."

Roger hesitated, then took one.

"Thanks."

"Why don't you relax here for a bit? You've had a pretty tough day," Philip said. "You look—"

He broke off, for the door opened. He turned round in annoyance, and his expression had the cold hostility that his father could show. The footman was in the doorway looking positively animated with distress.

"Redding, I told you—"

"I know, sir, I'm sorry, I just had to interrupt. It's Miss Barbara, she—she just telephoned. She says she's frightened, sir, *terrified* is the word she used.

She's been to the East End, phoned from a call box, and—she *screamed*, sir." The footman gulped. "And then she dropped the receiver, and—and someone hung up."

14

Disappearance

Roger was at the telephone, speaking to Turnbull.

"Get all patrol cars in the vicinity to converge on Brickett Street and the telephone kiosks in the area. Have every available man in AZ Division concentrated on the spot. Double the guard at Mulcaster's house; don't let anyone go in or out. If Miss Denny's picked up, radio the information. I'll be in my car and on the way."

"Oke." Turnbull was abrupt.

"Then telephone Chatworth and tell him. Then go to Brickett Street yourself," Roger said.

"Oke."

"Be seeing you." Roger rang off.

The footman was standing nervously at attention; Philip Sarkey was champing at the bit in the open doorway. Then suddenly he moved, disappeared, and caused a delay which didn't seem to make sense.

He shouted from another room, "You go on, I'll join you."

Roger didn't go on, but followed the sound of the

voice, found himself in the doorway of a bedroom, and saw Philip on his knees beside the open door of a huge wardrobe in a bedroom which was the last word in luxury. He was tugging and swearing at a drawer, got it open, then snatched up a gun. He didn't waste a second, but slid that into his pocket, took out a spare clip of ammunition, and pushed that into another pocket. Then he sprang up, turned, and was startled only for a second when he saw Roger.

"I'll teach the swine," he said. "Come on!"

The front door was open; the lift was waiting; the commissionaire was waiting at the street doors. Philip's Rolls-Bentley was now standing just in front of Roger's new Wolseley, and it made the pride of the Wests, mother, father, and sons, look like a midget model.

"Not yours—my car," Roger said.

"Not on your life! I—"

"I can contact the Yard and Divisions by radio, but please yourself." Roger reached his own car, hurt his left hand getting in, and then heard Philip by his side.

"All right, but for the love of heaven let me drive. With that hand—"

Roger slid across the front seat.

"Go ahead."

Philip didn't even grunt his thanks. His foot went down on the accelerator, the engine roared, the car shot forward, Roger felt his heart drop with a bump; concern for the car forced everything else out of his mind for a split second. It was soon gone, but he said:

"Don't tear its guts out."

"I'll buy you another," Philip rasped, and swung

round a corner with everything that could screech, screeching. Roger held tight, but took the radio telephone off its hook and held it; if a message were put out, he'd hear the voice and clap the ear-piece on. They reached Piccadilly.

Philip broke the silence suddenly.

"Sorry, West, ruddy insolent of me, but I'm so scared for Barbara I can hardly think."

"Forget it, but get us there alive. I've seen one accident today."

"I know what I'm doing, and I know the short cuts."

"Miss the one to the morgue."

Philip took his eyes off the road for a split second; only for a split second. Roger saw his lips quirk at the corners. Janet would say that what Philip Sarkey needed was an old-fashioned thrashing, or else something explosive, to jolt the arrogance out of him. But what hope was there with the son of such a father? At least he drove magnificently, his timing was superb, he ignored the speed limits but didn't put any other car or pedestrians in danger.

"Another thing," Roger said, near Ludgate Circus. "What the dickens do you think you're going to do with that gun?"

"Show me a man who's hurt Barbara, and—"

"I've met hot heads before, and they're as dangerous whether they're Irishmen, Scottish nationalists, or the sons of commercial tycoons," Roger growled. "I want prisoners, not corpses. Have you a license to carry firearms?"

"Like hell I have!"

"Well, forget to use the gun."

They turned a corner into a street which led through the city's dark streets, past the insurance offices and the head offices of big banks, and the center of the web of industry and commerce which spread throughout the world. The narrow, ill-lit thoroughfare was empty, and they touched seventy, horn blaring at every corner.

At the junction with Aldgate, near the pump which had seen centuries of hurrying men, Philip said:

"Okay. I'll keep my head."

Roger didn't answer.

They were at Brickett Street before he realized it. A policeman, stolidly crossing the road, leaped out of the way. There was a crowd; concentrate the police in the East End, and there would be either a big crowd hampering, jeering, sneering—or no one about at all. At least a hundred people were lining the curbs at the corners, but the police had kept them away from Brickett Street itself.

Then a bell shrilled out with an unmistakable urgency, and Philip Sarkey, sliding the car to a standstill, stalled the engine and made the car jolt.

An ambulance turned the corner ahead.

"Oh, God, no," Philip groaned.

The ambulance stopped outside Number 28, the Mulcasters' house.

Big Sopley of AZ Division was actually standing on the pavement by the side of the ambulance, when Roger got out of the car. He was on the near side; Philip had to come from the road.

"Who is it?" Roger asked sharply.

"Eh? Who—oh, Handsome. Don't know for sure, but he's as dead as mutton. Had to clear out to let the ambulance men get in. A neighbor's in with the Mulcaster girl."

Philip came rushing and heard the last words, stopped short, and drew in his breath with a whistling sound that made such an odd, high pitch that Sopley and everyone else turned to look at him. Then he said gratingly:

"Who killed her? Come on, tell me, who—"

Sopley said, "What have we got here? Didn't come with you, Handsome, did it?"

Tell me who killed her! roared Philip.

"A man's been killed," Roger said quietly, "and if you can't keep your head better than this, go and hold up a bar." He was deliberately harsh, believed it would do the man good. "You say you don't know who it is, Sop?"

"Some red-haired chap. Lucky thing we came here, it looked like being a bloody massacre. Apparently—"

It sounded like O'Leary.

"Any news of Miss Denny?"

Sopley said, "No, haven't seen a trace, haven't heard a word. Not since she left here."

"So she came by herself," Philip muttered.

"Apparently. Why don't these do-gooders learn sense?" Sopley didn't know who the other man was, and wouldn't have cared if he had. "She had a chat with Rosie Mulcaster, and then went off. Our chap watching in the store saw her. She was here for about twenty minutes alone with Rosie— at least, we thought she was alone. Mulcaster and this other chap—"

"The man named O'Leary, sir," put in a plain-clothes man.

"Oh, that fellow?" Sopley showed no surprise. "I've been off this afternoon, wouldn't have been here myself at all if I hadn't looked in at the station to check a pickup we had this evening. Well, Mulcaster and this other chap were up at the Red Bull. They came back and went into Number 28 ten minutes after Miss Denny had left. Next thing our chaps knew, there was a hell of a do. Three or four shots came from the door—two bullets lodged in O'Leary's face, one in our chap in the street. But the copper picked himself up and tried to get in, didn't lose much time. The killer went out the back way. And that's where we come unstuck," Sopley went on gloomily. "Our chap watching the back was taken by surprise. Didn't stop the killer, who knocked him out and vanished."

"Let's get this right," said Roger. "Mulcaster and O'Leary came in. Someone was waiting inside, K.O.'d Mulcaster, killed O'Leary, shot the street policeman at the back, and then K.O.'d your other policeman."

Sopley wrinkled his nose.

"Sounds a bit bald, said like that, but that's the size of it. Don't forget he had the advantage of surprise."

Roger said, "Yes, I suppose so."

Philip Sarkey, a few yards away, was speaking to a uniformed man, demanding news.

"Who's your pal?" Sopley asked.

"Miss Denny's boy friend."

"This young love!" Sopley sniffed. "Well, the killer got clear away, and made us a present of the gun—threw it into the gutter. By the time our chaps broke in, Rosie was bending over her precious husband, moaning, and the mess—"

Sopley broke off.

The ambulance men came out of 28 Brickett Street, carrying a stretcher. A third man was at the open doors at the back of the ambulance. The man on the stretcher was covered from head to foot, but the top of his head showed, and the street lamps glowed on the coppery hair. Then the stretcher was put smoothly inside.

"We can go in now," Sopley said, moving his great bulk toward the narrow front door. He didn't get in first, though; Philip Sarkey pushed past him, actually knocking him off his balance. He glowered and grabbed, but Roger held his arm back.

The gas light was dull in the little front room.

Rosie wasn't in here. Billy was; stretched out, unconscious. A chair had been pushed aside, a table knocked over, a glass vase broken. On the threadbare carpet there were patches which looked like blood which had soaked well in. A plain-clothes man was on his knees with a steel tape, another was busy with a tripod and camera.

Philip said, "Where's that girl?" He rushed across the foot of the stairs with Roger on his heels. Roger saw Rosie over his shoulder, then saw Philip stop, as if he had collided with an invisible wall.

A woman was bending over Rosie, who was sitting up in an old-fashioned saddle-back armchair, opening her eyes, looking dazedly about her. Suddenly she cried;

"Where's *Billy?*"

"Your Billy's all right, dear," soothed the woman with her, and she glared at Philip. "What the hell do you want, can't you see she's too ill to see anyone?"

The man did not seem to hear. He dropped on

one knee, took Rosie's hands, and peered up into the pale face.

"Listen, Rosie, what happened to Barbara?" he begged. "What happened to Miss Denny? If you know anything, tell me. You've got to tell me."

She didn't answer.

Sopley looked at the kneeling man, and then at Roger, with his eyebrows raised. The woman glared viciously at Philip's lion's mane. Rosie seemed more dazed than frightened, more puzzled than worried; she wasn't really herself yet.

Then a plain-clothes man came in.

"Excuse me, sir. Miss Denny's car has just been found—half submerged in an old backwater near Tivvy Docks."

There was utter silence. In it, Philip Sarkey's head raised slowly.

When he looked into the man's eyes, Roger wondered whether anything could keep him sane.

"Come on, Sarkey," Roger said brusquely. "Turnbull, you keep close to Mulcaster; I want to talk to him. I'd like to be quite sure that there was a third man in the house," he added grimly.

Sopley didn't make a squeak. Philip followed Roger out without a word.

15

The Body in the Car

The headlamps of cars were turned toward the sheet of water near Tivvy Docks. Two searchlights had been rigged up on near-by warehouses, and shone down upon the dark, smooth, smelly stretch of water. Two old, disused warehouses, little more than walls of rubble, were close to the quayside where the men worked.

A mobile crane was already in position, grinding as it turned round.

Roger and Philip Sarkey watched as the men worked—lightermen from the main docks, not far away. Each man moved quickly yet with deliberation; each knew exactly what he had to do.

One was in a swim suit, in spite of the autumn cold, and standing on the gunwale of an old lighter, the only craft near by. Tivvy Docks had been out of use for years; they had once served a brewery which had shifted its main premises. It had a bad reputation for seepage and silting up, and had never been taken over. It was half a mile from railway lines, too, and difficult to approach from railway lines, too, and difficult to approach by road—part of the old dockside area of the middle nineteenth century. On foot, one had to approach it by a flight of narrow stone steps; and although cars could be brought up to the edge of the old, collapsing quayside, there was no short cut to the other side because of new docks which had been built to oust Tivvy's.

The light was yellow, eerie, glaring.

Philip Sarkey was standing near Roger, intent on the man who was preparing to dive. His task was simple: he was to take a rope and loop it round the back wheels of the car, a Hillman sedan, which were just touching the water. Once that was done, it would be out of the water in a matter of minutes, and they could see whether anyone was inside.

Philip had said practically nothing since they had left Brickett Street; just given a grunt or two. Hands in pockets, big jaw thrust forward, powerful shoulders surging right and left, he had walked from the spot where they had left the cars. Roger could imagine his feelings; in fact, Roger himself found it hard not to think of the tall, well-dressed woman with her grace and her looks.

Dead?

Now the diver poised on the side of the old lighter, then made a shallow dive. He made hardly a splash. A few yards away, a man said, "Rather him than me, it's perishing cold." Roger hadn't noticed the cold. Philip, hands still in his pockets, stared at the rippling water as the diver went under for a moment, rope in his hands; then bobbed up and, in a couple of strokes, reached the other side of the car and looped the rope round that wheel. He swam away from the half-submerged car, and waved.

"Okay!" he called.

He began to swim toward the steps, where men were waiting for him with towels and blankets. His body looked very white against the black surface. The car itself must have struck something, perhaps silt at the bottom of the backwater, for it was tilted at a sharp angle. The number plate and rear wheels were above water, and part of the roof as well as the back of the car. The front was submerged, and there was no way of telling whether anyone was in it until it was raised.

The engine of the crane began to turn, making ugly, rasping noises. Men called out. The crane began to tug at the rope, pulling it out of the water, then dragging it taut. Soon it began to hoist the car. It was just possible to see the black water ripple.

Roger found himself gritting his own teeth.

Philip was breathing through his nostrils with a whistling sound; his teeth were set and oddly bared, lips turned back. A savage, snarling lion.

The engine roared louder; the crane seemed to snarl, too.

All of the back of the car was lifted clear, and the crane swung round a little, then began to drag the nose of the car through the water toward the side. A gang of men was waiting with hooks, more ropes and tackle. Every face, every feature, every ripple, and every drop of water showed plainly in the glare of the headlamps and the searchlights.

Then the rope broke.

The car crashed bodily into the water. A great wave came up, drenching the men on the quayside, splashing Roger and Philip as far as their knees. There was a grinding sound, and the car slithered, moving forward with water thrashing about it. The engine of the crane cut out. One man was cursing, most just looked sick, several stared at Philip.

"The clumsy, ruddy fools," Philip muttered viciously, then tore off his topcoat and dived in.

A man cried, "He'll kill himself; it's only a few feet deep!"

It must have been more than a few feet. Philip hit the water with a belly flop, caused a great splash and big wave, then struck out toward the car. Every stroke he made was clearly visible. Each time he raised his arms, water dripped from his sodden sleeves, and he kept tossing his head back, shaking water off it. But he hurled himself forward, and seemed oblivious of his clothes.

Barbara Denny's car was now submerged almost to roof level; men could see only the tops of the windows; and it appeared to be standing on all four wheels.

Close to the front of the car, Philip Sarkey seemed to heave himself out of the water, and then to dive. He disappeared. Bubbles appeared and water rippled, loud in the hush of watching men. Nothing seemed to happen for a long time. The first diver, still at the foot of the steps, poised himself to go in, but as he raised his arms, Roger saw Philip's head break the surface. He'd only come up for air; and did that twice again before treading water.

Then he began to swim toward the steps. The men there were waiting to help him up. Something he had discovered had made a big difference to him. Roger could tell that as he saw him coming up the steps swiftly, shaking his great lion's mane, ugly face touched with a kind of calmness.

"She isn't in it," he said to Roger. "A man is, but Barbara isn't. I felt the head; it's a man. We've got to find her. Get that, West? We've got to find her. Spend money like water, use every bloody man you've got, but find her. Understand, *find her.*"

"It's the one thing we're going to do," Roger said.

He didn't speak of dragging the backwater then, and Philip Sarkey didn't seem to realize the possibility that Barbara's body might yet be somewhere in that dark pool.

It wasn't; they knew that for certain an hour later.

Roger went back to the Mulcasters' house. Turnbull was still there, so angry that he seemed hardly interested in the news from Tivvy's Docks. He behaved like this only when he had made a terrific effort but failed utterly. So Rosie and her Billy were a match for him.

Neither looked it. Mulcaster was now sitting up, head bruised but not badly hurt, and reasonably self-assured.

"He could have got those bruises banging his head against a wall," Turnbull growled. "I think he's been foxing."

"You mustn't say it!" Rosie cried. "Billy, say something, tell them what happened."

"He hasn't said a word," Turnbull rasped.

Billy Mulcaster stirred. He didn't look at Rosie or at Turnbull, only at West.

"I came in with O'Leary," he said. "A guy shot at us. I thought you cops was watching."

Roger didn't speak.

The youth was tight-lipped, and his face was touched with a kind of ugliness. He didn't say another thing. It would be a waste of time trying to make him. There was nothing Roger would like better than to get tough with Mulcaster, but not only was Mulcaster cunning; there was poor, despairing, frightened Rosie.

"I think you'd better come and talk at the station, Mulcaster," Roger said, gruffly. "Come with him, Sergeant." This would please Turnbull, anyhow. "If he's done nothing, Mrs. Mulcaster, you needn't worry."

They left Rosie with a neighbor.

Nothing they could say or do could alter Mulcaster's story. They had to let him go.

"We can't find any traces but there could have been a third man in the house," Roger agreed. "Someone who wanted to kill O'Leary and Mulcaster." He brooded; then: "Exactly what did Rosie say?"

"She was next door when the shooting started," Turnbull told him. "She heard it and rushed into the house after the copper had forced the front door. That's all about the shooting. She talked freely enough about what happened earlier. Barbara Denny had been to see her, apparently convinced that Rosie had sent a man to telephone a message asking the Denny woman to come at once. Rosie swore she didn't know anything about it."

Neighbors and a policeman had seen her car parked round the corner. Others had seen her drive off. No one could help, beyond that; no one had seen her car near Tivvy's Docks.

Barbara Denny's maid confirmed that her mistress had received a telephone call from a man with a rough voice. Barbara had not said where she was going, just that she would be gone two hours or so. The timing was right, too.

There was no news of Barbara from any London Division.

There was no news of the prewar Packard, either.

It was after one o'clock when Roger finally drove away from Brickett Street. Turnbull had already left. Roger maneuvered his left hand more easily; there was little traffic on the road and nothing to worry about.

He went to the Yard, telephoned AZ Division HQ, and picked up several reports; all were negative. It wasn't really a safe thing to say that because they hadn't found her body Barbara Denny wasn't dead, but if the attackers had wanted to kill her, wouldn't that have been the easiest way?

The submerged car was up now, and the dead man had been taken out. He was shortish, with a very big stomach, huge shoulders, and a big chest. On the young side of middle age. There had been nothing about his body or on his clothes to help identification, but by the morning photographs would be distributed, and with luck the police would know who he was within twenty-four hours.

About the only place where nothing unusual had happened that night was Pretzel's Restaurant, judging from the reports.

Roger stared with heavy eyes at the mass of notes and reports, then started to get up. He'd have to get some rest. The telephone bell rang before he could leave the desk.

"Hallo?"

"Sir Gerald Sarkey is here, sir, and would like you to see him," the operater said.

"Sir *Gerald?* Not Mr. Philip?"

"No, sir, Sir Gerald."

"I see," said Roger. "Yes, all right, have him brought up."

Sarkey came in, moving swiftly. Roger had an odd impression: that he was a younger, sprightlier man. All the cold aloofness had gone, the absolute self-control had been relaxed.

"West, I've just heard what's happened. My son telephoned me. Do you know if Barbara—" He didn't finish.

So Barbara really mattered to him.

Roger said heavily, "I'm hoping to have word about her at any minute, Sir Gerald."

"I hope to God that's true," Sarkey said. "If anything should happen—" He broke off, and the aloofness came back; it was as if his years fell upon him. "I am prepared to offer a very big reward to help find her. Any figure you like. Do everything, try everything—"

"We shall do that in any case, sir," Roger said. "It's too early to talk about a reward. I hope it

154

won't be necessary. Where can I find you, if news comes?"

"I shall be at my son's flat, at Parable Court," Sarkey said.

Roger saw him to the door. Sarkey didn't say another word; only his eyes gave him away. This cold, aloof, arrogant man was desperately frightened, was no more proof against the ordinary emotions than any man or woman.

What did he feel toward his missing ward? A guardian's affection, or something much stronger?

Roger went downstairs to his car.

Twenty minutes later he turned into Bell Street. There was no lighted window in the whole street, and only three street lamps. He slowed down. Philip Sarkey did not appear to have damaged the car, which was running sweetly and smoothly. Janet would be asleep, with luck, and the boys for certain.

He walked up the drive to open the garage doors; when he was out, Janet liked them closed, to fool anyone looking for an easy place to burgle. Who could blame her? Then he heard the telephone bell ringing in the house, cursed the caller, and moved swiftly toward the front door. When he opened it the ringing had stopped; he could hear Janet speaking upstairs.

16

Warning and Threat

Roger pushed the door behind him and it slammed. He heard Janet break off, and then she called down to him, "Is that you?" He shouted back and hurried up the stairs, hearing her speak into the telephone, catching the words: "He's coming in now." As he strode into the bedroom, kneeing the door wide open, she hitched herself up in the big double bed and looked flushed, drowsy, and good to see.

"It's that beast Turnbull." She held out the telephone.

"He wouldn't call if it weren't necessary."

"I think he'd call if it was only to wake you up."

Roger grinned, dropped onto the side of the bed, and took the telephone. Janet saw his bandaged fingers. He grimaced at her, leaned forward and kissed her nose, then said:

"Hallo, Warren?"

"I'm just plain mad at myself worrying you again tonight," Turnbull said, "but I couldn't avoid it. It's either this, or that raving lunatic called Philip Sarkey on your doorstep. I wouldn't be surprised if he doesn't drag Chatworth out of bed to tell him about it."

"What's he up to now?"

Turnbull said more soberly, "Well, being honest, I can understand it. I went back with him to his swell apartment as he hadn't got his car, and he asked me in for a drink. I thought I might pick something up, so I said okay. He had a telephone call from someone he didn't know, while I was there, and nearly passed out."

"Threats?" Roger asked heavily.

"And how! Mr. Anonymous has got his Barbara. Young Sarkey's to lay off the police and just wait for instructions. She'll be all right while he does what he's told, but if he disobeys, anything might happen to her; she's a very attractive woman. You know the kind of vicious stuff," Turnbull went on. "Do nothing but wait until he hears again."

Roger didn't speak.

Janet was now sitting quite straight, and much of her tiredness seemed to have gone. She was studying Roger's face, and kept glancing at the bandaged fingers.

"You still there?" asked Turnbull.

"Yes, I'm still here. So Philip Sarkey turned this over to you right away."

"He didn't have much chance. I was with him, remember, when he was right off his balance, and once he knew he couldn't keep it from me, he blew up. Incompetent dolts, what do we think we are?—everything as per," Turnbull went on. "I said I'd ring you, and he said—"

The line went dead.

"You there?" asked Roger, sharply.

"Roger, it doesn't matter what it is, you've got to stop talking, and take it easy," Janet broke in. "You look dreadful."

"I'm all right, make me a cuppa, darling. Turnbull, are you there?" The line still sounded dead. "I don't—"

"Hallo," another man said. "Hallo, is Chief inspector West there?" It wasn't Turnbull's voice.

"Who the hell's that? I was speaking to—"

"Sorry, Handsome, it's Sopley here," said the AZ Superintendent. "I persuaded the exchange to cut you off the other call and put me through. I think we know where the Denny girl is."

That went through Roger like a knife.

"Go on."

"Got her through that Packard you were so damned anxious to find," Sopley told him. "Haven't time to talk; I'm on my way there. A garage in Webb Street, near the Rialto, first turning—"

"Webb Street, Whitechapel?" Roger barked.

"Yes."

"I know it. I'm coming. 'By." Roger hung up and stood up in one movement.

Everything that Janet could find in the way of disapproval was in her expression, and yet he didn't really notice.

"Darling," he said, "it's just one of those things. I always knew that when this started to break, it would break with a bang. I've got to go."

"If you leave this house before you've had something to eat and drink—"

"I've been eating and drinking all day. Sorry, sweet."

Janet said, almost with anguish, "It's your food

158

and drink, it's the air you breathe, it's your wife and children, it's your blood and your bed. Oh, how I hate it!"

Roger stopped moving and looked down at her. His heart was banging. The bedside light was kind to her, taking the years away; she was the young woman who had first waited for him, sitting as she was now, some fourteen years ago. Except for her closed eyes, that was, and her hopeless expression and her pale face.

He went forward and took her hands.

"Listen, Jan, it's been a hell of a day. They've killed a man, and now they've kidnaped a woman. You'd like her. She got into it, God knows why, because she wanted to help a girl whose father was murdered. It's my job, just as much as it would be yours if one of the boys caught a packet and I wasn't here to help. It's my *job*."

After a long time, Janet opened her eyes.

"Yes," she said, "yes, I know. I'm sorry. It was being waked up so suddenly, I'll be all right. You'd better—you'd better hurry."

When she heard the car moving along Bell Street, she was crying.

About an hour earlier, P.C. Bigglesworth of the AZ Division, a man in his late twenties, comparatively new to the Force but fresh from the army and ready to have a go at anything that might bring early promotion, passed the Excel Garage in Webb Street, Whitechapel. It was the third time he had passed it within the hour, although he knew that he was taking a chance because he had soon to meet his sergeant at a rendezvous ten minutes' walk away. He passed this time to make sure that the old Packard wasn't there. If it was, he could see it through a window in the big shed which served as a garage.

The memo about a Packard, prewar and probably 1937, -8, or -9 manufacture, had been on the notice board at the station. Bigglesworth had read it, and immediately thought of the car which Nick White garaged here. Nick White wasn't a man anyone liked. He ran the garage as a secondary job; he was also a bookmaker, who used the Packard for journeys to race tracks all over the country. He had several clerks, and the Packard carried them all, with the boards, cards, books, and cash; all the paraphernalia of course betting.

Nick White often had a big sum of ready money, but he'd never had trouble with it.

The Packard sometimes returned late at night from places in the Midlands and the North; occasionally it wasn't home until dawn.

The night before last—that is, the night of the Jefferson's store murder—it hadn't come in until the early hours of the morning. Bigglesworth hadn't seen it arrive, but he'd since checked and found that it wasn't there at four, but had been at six.

It wasn't there now.

"Pity," he said, and looked along the long, white road, with its lamp posts and tiny lights, its silent houses, its chimneys silhouetted against a starlit sky. "I'd better tell the sarge."

He stepped out of the builder's yard, from which he could keep watch on the garage. As he did so, a car turned out of the main road with its side lights on. It sprang to Bigglesworth's mind that this might be the Packard, and he darted back behind

160

the gateway of the yard. Next moment, headlights shone out, stretching right along the street and reflecting on the windows of the tiny houses, showing the sickly yellow paint of the two petrol pumps, and a big tin tire advertisement.

The engine ran smoothly; the tires purred.

The car slowed down.

Bigglesworth, who spent a lot of time plodding the streets and working out what he would do in an emergency, took off his helmet and peered over the fence. He kept by a post, so that he was less likely to be seen.

The two men were in the car.

One jumped out and went to open the big doors of the corrugated-iron garage. The other opened a back door of the car and leaned inside. He was like that for some time, just his legs and rump showing, dark trousers stretched tightly.

Then the other man came back, cursing.

"There's the big Humber in the way; we can't get in."

The man withdrew from the car.

"They didn't think we'd get back," he said. "Okay—we'll have to take her in."

He bent down inside the Packard again. Soon he began to gasp and grunt; then he pulled at something heavy, backing away gradually. In a muted voice, he said:

"Get a move on, Charlie."

Bigglesworth straightened his legs as he watched, and his heart began to thump. What was in the back of the car? The swag? Were they really crooks, coming back from a job?

Everything he had heard about the Gelignite Gang came to his mind.

161

To get a better view, he stepped cautiously onto a stack of wood.

There was no sign of Nick White.

The two men were working together now, one at each rear door; one was pushing, the other, with his back to the policeman, pulling. They kept grunting. Whatever it was jammed the doorway. Suddenly Bigglesworth heard a muttered comment that made his heart give a wild bound.

"The long-legged bitch, she—"

"Shut your trap!"

"She" meant a woman; not the car.

The men fell silent.

Bigglesworth felt suffocated as he thought of the message brought by the sergeant on his last round; the search for a woman—what was her name? Denny. The description included the vital phrase: Height, 5 ft. 10 in. And these men were getting a long-legged woman out of the car.

He craned his neck.

Yes, it was a woman.

The man with his back to Bigglesworth had her shoulders, and pulled her out of the car, letting her legs drop onto the concrete yard with a dull sound. The light of a distant street lamp showed the shiny luster of her hair: Bigglesworth saw her face, with the high-bridged nose, the high forehead.

The other man came round from the other side of the car.

"Okay," he said, "I'll take her feet. I—"

He broke off.

He had been facing the fence a few feet away from the watching policeman.

Bigglesworth was quite sure he had been seen. He saw the man, half bending to get a grip on the

162

girl's legs, stop as abruptly as he stopped speaking. Then saw his right hand move toward his hip pocket.

Bigglesworth leaped off his perch, snatched his whistle, and blew with tremendous force. The noise screamed into the quiet night. Legs moving like pistons, whistle at his lips, truncheon in his hand, Bigglesworth leaped toward the gateway and across the road. Opposite, there was a low brick wall in front of the terraced houses.

He heard the roar of a shot, and a bullet smashed a window.

He was too excited to be really scared, and was wondering wildly if he had a chance to keep the men there or whether they'd run for it. They wouldn't have time to go off in the car, would they? They'd have to leave the prisoner behind.

And that girl?

Then Bigglesworth had his one prayed-for break.

A police patrol car swung into Webb Street; he could see the illuminated POLICE sign, and hear its racing engine. He flung himself down behind the wall as another shot roared. The bullet struck the bricks just in front of his head. He dared to raise his head, saw the two men together in a moment of indecision, then saw one of them turn and run away from the direction of the police car.

The other quickly hoisted the woman to his shoulders, and staggered toward the open garage door. Bigglesworth shouted, leaped over the wall and rushed forward, his truncheon swinging. A man appeared at the garage door and shot the policeman. Bigglesworth pitched forward, pain killing surprise.

The man carrying Barbara Denny disappeared

into the garage; the man with the gun closed the sliding doors.

The patrol car drew up.

The driver jumped out, as the man next to him finished his radio flash to the Division.

17

The Garage

Crooks barricading themselves in and threatening to give battle had happened often enough in the past, and would happen often enough again. Roger had been through several desperate fights. There was something different about each one, but each had a menacing note of uncertainty; would the trapped men kill or would they release the prisoner? Most submitted after a show of defiance, but the men at the garage were known associates of killers.

He weighed up the position quickly.

The corrugated-iron garage was a little affair, next to a builders' yard in a fairly wide road. On the other side of the garage was a small house, the front of which was obviously a shop, selling accessories. The house stood on its own, a tiny oasis of bricks and mortar. One wall, that which ran alongside the wall of the garage, was absolutely blank. The other three walls of the house had plenty of windows or doors. It was impossible to approach it without being seen; one could sense the unseen, watching men.

Two pumps outside the garage showed up bilious yellow in the glare of headlamps, and Roger felt as if he had been through all this once before tonight. There were as many police, more cars, even a few night birds watching curiously.

And there was big, ungainly Sopley, with his pipe.

"Nothing new, yet," Sopley said when he saw Roger. "You haven't brought Conquering Hero Sarkey with you, I hope? We don't want any more Tarzan tricks."

"Sure it's Barbara Denny?"

"Well, pretty sure," said Sopley. "It was the lookout for the Packard that did it. Had a live man on this beat, and he knew a Packard was garaged here, owned by a bookie, often out late. He noticed that it was out earlier tonight, so kept a special watch. It turned up about half an hour before I phoned you. He was actually on the spot. He saw two men lift something out of the car, and was all worked up when he saw it was a woman."

Roger said, "Fine."

"He was in the builder's yard there." Sopley jerked his pipe. "Got a bullet in his side, but he's not in danger."

"When it's over, I'll have a word with him," Roger promised. He paused. "If that house was a pillbox, it couldn't be harder to get at."

"You're telling me," Sopley said. "Well, they're in there. Three men, maybe more, and the woman. They went in through the garage, a patrol nipped round and saw 'em going in at the back door. We've got a job on."

"Tried to talk to the men inside yet?"

"We've called to them but they haven't answered. Two lads went up to the front door, and were fired on; I pulled 'em off pretty quick. Still, we've got the place surrounded, and one of my D.I.'s is working out a plan of attack. Don't want any heroics, Handsome; I like to keep my men alive. And I mean *my* chaps."

"I want her alive," Roger said.

"All I'm saying," emphasized Sopley, "is that I want to take all the precautions I can. I don't want my chaps to go throwing their lives away. Young Bigglesworth came near enough to it."

Roger said, "What's the layout?"

"There's the garage, really just a big shed, and the shop and the flat above the shop." Sopley pointed. "The flat's got a separate entrance. The shop and showroom's separate, too, and there's no way to the flat from outside. They've got the flat windows manned, to keep us from getting anywhere near."

"*All* windows manned?"

"Don't know for certain, but they can see pretty well everything we do. We could rush 'em, but they'll get tired before we do, Handsome. They won't play any tricks with the girl, either. They'll know it will go too hard on them if they do. Patience, that's what we want now—patience with a capital P. *No* deeds of derring-do."

"You're a timid old so-and-so," Roger said, but he grinned.

He didn't feel tired now.

A fire tender came up, half a dozen men on it wearing steel helmets. They started to unroll the big hoses, and to connect them with a hydrant. An ambulance was standing by. Sopley hadn't left anything to chance. The difficulty was to judge the mood of the men inside. They'd shot Bigglesworth, they'd shot at other policemen, they'd killed O'Leary, they'd killed old Maitland.

Roger finished a circuit of the house and garage. Shadowy figures watched from the windows.

"Satisfied?" asked Sopley, dryly.

"Let me talk to them, will you?"

"Please yourself." They were by the side of a police car with a public-address outfit. Roger didn't have to get inside, but took the microphone and leaned against the open car door, looking at the dark house, the closed windows. The microphone began to whistle; it was live.

"What's the name of the garage owner?"

"White. Nick for Nicholas White."

"Thanks. Hallo, there," Roger called, and his voice came loud and distinctly, up and down the street, waking more people from their beds, startling others who were already at their windows and doorways, or seeping onto the pavement. "Hallo, White! This is the police calling. We want to talk to you."

There was no answer; no sign of life.

"We know you can hear us," Roger called. "Don't make fools of yourselves. Give yourself up, and bring the woman out unhurt. You'll get a square deal. Throw your guns out of the window first."

Only silence and darkness greeted him.

Roger waited for two minutes.

"White, you're only wasting your time. You'll get badly hurt if you make a fight of it. We can call troops out, if necessary; your toy pistols won't be any good against machine guns. Open a window,

throw your guns out, then come and give yourselves up. It will go easier for you if you do."

He stopped.

Then he jumped, half scared, and every other policeman near by started. There was a jerky movement about the crowd; every head turned sharply,
and everyone seemed suddenly affected by a nervous tick.

"Now it's my turn," a man called over another
public-address outfit. His voice boomed, the sound
buffeted the ears and seemed to echo against the
roofs and the windows of the tiny terrace houses.
*"Listen to me, coppers. If you want this woman alive,
let me and my men go, see. All of us."*

The booming faded.

Silence fell.

Sopley took his pipe from his lips, and Roger
thought with savage disappointment, "They all try
it, what idiocy gets into them?" There wasn't a
case on record of the police doing that kind of deal
with trapped men, but time and time and time
again it was tried. Perhaps desperation made
White and the others believe that they had a
chance, after all. Probably they knew subcon-
sciously that nothing could save them from the
gallows, and they had to try fantastic methods.
One deadly possibility remained: that they knew
they'd hang when caught, so they might harm
Barbara Denny, in that desperate, futile attempt to
save themselves; or they might harm her out of
malice.

"Well, what about it?" the man boomed.

Roger called, "White, you know you haven't a
chance. Give it up. Don't do any more harm to that
woman. Throw your guns—"

"Oh, go to hell." The booming voice held a note of anger. *"Give us free passage, or we'll cut off her ears and throw them down."*

A shiver ran through the crowd.

The worst thing of all was the tone of the man's voice. Some men threatened nervously, screwing themselves up to make a challenge; their nerve would break when it came to the point of carrying out the threat. And there was the man, the really bad man, who meant exactly what he said.

This man meant what he said.

Sopley put a hand on Roger's arm.

"Handsome," he said flatly, "he's liable to do it."

"Yes," agreed Roger, tautly. "Have the firemen get ready down the street, will you, out of sight. Have them get well set, then forward with hoses at the ready, one to be trained on each window. If we can drench them in the rooms, we might make it. How long will the firemen take?"

"Dunno. Jimmy!" Sopley called sharply to a fire-brigade man talking to two uniformed policemen. "Here a minute. How long will it take to . . ."

The brigade chief answered brusquely, "Ten minutes."

"Get cracking, will you?" Roger said, then flicked the mike on again. His voice changed, too, became high pitched, sounded as if he were worried. "White, can you hear me? White!"

"I can hear you, and you can hear me. She's got nice little ears."

"Listen, White, you mustn't do it! She hasn't done you any harm." Policemen, firemen, and people from the houses as well as several reporters there were thrusting their way toward the police cars; many felt a twinge of disgust at the scared

170

tone of Roger's voice. "We can't let you go, not on our own authority; we'll have to refer to Scotland Yard. But don't hurt that woman, don't—"

"I'll give you five minutes," boomed the man in the flat above the garage. *"Nice little ears she's got, I've just had a look."*

Inside the flat, neither of the voices sounded as loud as they did outside. Roger's was much louder than the other man's, Nick White's. White's words reached Barbara Denny's ears clearly but faintly, as if he were talking in another room. He wasn't. He was sitting at a small table, with a microphone on a stand, and the equipment for the loud-speaker system behind him, neatly arranged wires and a few boxes, coils and things which Barbara didn't recognize. He was a smallish man with a narrow face and very black hair, a pronounced widow's peak, dark eyelashes, a pointed chin. He wore a well-fitting suit of navy blue, and looked brisk and businesslike. Now and again he glanced at Barbara but he wasn't really interested in her.

Another man, who had watched her when she had been in the telephone kiosk, who had scared her then and absolutely terrified her when he had forced her to stop her car in a dark, narrow street, came in from another room. She knew there were three or four other men here, at the windows, watching.

The first man here, White, said to the newcomer, "You get the Blower?"

"Yeh. He said he's sent someone, they're on the way."

"They'd better hurry." White took out a gold cigarette case and lit a cigarette. He glanced at Bar-

171

bara. She was in a corner on the floor. They dragged her up the stairs and into this room, and flung her here. She had come round as they had dragged her, realized what they were doing, felt the pain as she had been bumped on stair after stair. They had seen that she was conscious, but hadn't taken any notice, just flung her down. She was lying on one side, her whole body aching with pain, and her mind filled with the anguish of fear.

It was the coldness of White's voice which struck the deepest terror into her.

It had something of the timbre of Gerald Sarkey's. It was flat and expressionless, and seemed to convey exactly what was in the man's mind; nothing was likely to make him bend one way or the other.

Twice, he glanced at her head; at her *ears*.

The other man looked at her, but not in the same way. He was of much poorer metal, a brute with brute strength and a brute's animal courage. The gun bulged in his pocket.

Yet he was edgy.

"Supposing the Blower doesn't play ball," he said.

The man named White drew at his cigarette.

"He will. He knows I can name him. He knows if he lets me down, I'll tell the police everything there is to know. So he'll send help." Nick White stood up slowly, still drawing at the cigarette, and moved across to Barbara. Her body stiffened, and she wanted to cringe away. He stared at her expressionlessly as he finished: "He'll send a couple of the boys with a nice big tin of gelignite, and blow those ruddy cops to hell."

Barbara heard every syllable.

For the first time, something besides her own plight, her own danger, seeped into her mind.

"What a job for the Blower!" the other man exclaimed. "So long as he gets a move on."

"They'll soon be here," White said. "It won't go wrong. And we can always buy plenty of time. Did you hear how that copper squealed? Know who it is?"

"It looks like West to me."

"It's time West caught a packet," White said thinly. "And it'll hurt, when this one catches him." He gave a tight-lipped smile as he looked down at Barbara; and she returned his gaze—somehow she couldn't look away. His pale gray eyes seemed to take on an expression, now, of cruelty.

He bent down.

"Too bad you like slumming," he sneered. "Too bad you didn't learn to keep your aristocratic nose out of other people's business." His thin hands moved; he pressed her head down on the floor and pushed her thick, shining hair away from her right ear. She went rigid with terror. "That five minutes up yet, Boy?"

"I—I dunno. Listen, Nick, give them another two or three minutes."

White said, "You getting soft? Well, I'm not. If West gets one of her ears slapped in his face, he'll know we mean business, and be a hell of a sight more careful. He'll be expecting a rush out of here, won't he? He won't expect a car to drive up, or a couple of men to come and toss a load of gelignite among the crowd of cops, will he? It'll be like a ten-ton bomb on a Band of Hope meeting!" White's lips turned back as he sneered, and Barbara, terror gnawing at her, saw the tension on his face and

173

knew that he was fighting for self-control but was really as frightened as the man he called Boy.

"You know best," Boy muttered.

"I'm glad you concede me that. What's your knife like?"

"It—I dunno—"

"There's a razor in the bathroom," White said, "an old cutthroat. Ted used to use it. Go get it." He paused. "Put the light out."

"Okay."

"And check with the others—they're to bellow out if anything moves."

"Okay," Boy said.

He disappeared; in a moment, the sound of muttering voices came.

Barbara was caught in a violent fit of shivering. The word "razor" had done more than anything else to terrify her. She was not afraid simply because it might happen; she was sure that it would. She could almost feel the sharp, slicing pain as the blade cut. But terror did not paralyze her, and her mind had room for other horrors. This man, the Blower, was on his way with explosives, would maim and kill the police outside; and they wouldn't suspect the danger, would be taken completely by surprise. The man White hadn't said so, but obviously he believed that he, Boy, and the others could get away in the confusion. The callousness of it didn't affect Barbara so much as the horror.

A car might come at any minute, bringing that disaster.

White stood up.

Boy put out the light as he left the room, but a glow came from the landing. White moved away from Barbara. They had no more thought for her than they would have had for an animal; they didn't even allow the possibility that she could do anything; they had given her the ultimate insult of assuming she would just lie there, cowed.

White moved across the darkened room. She guessed that he was going to the window and, a moment later, knew that she was right. He pulled aside a curtain, and light came into the room from the street. She hadn't dreamed that the street would be so bright. She could see White standing close to the wall, looking out.

What could he see?

He couldn't see *her*.

She began to move, very slowly, filled with desperate fear of making a noise. Her body was weak, her muscles seemed to have wasted away. She gritted her teeth as she placed the palms of her hands against the floor and tried to hoist herself up. Her arms quivered violently, pain screamed through one elbow, and she dropped with a thud.

White did not even turn to look at her.

Outside, the police cars were lining the street, five of them in all. White could look down on the shiny roofs, and on the red and brass of a fire engine, some dark-clad figures, standing around as if doing nothing. Police and firemen were the same —he'd foxed them. It didn't occur to him that some men were preparing feverishly to raid the house.

There was Sopley, the fat slug, with a younger man—it might be West; White didn't know West except from his photographs, and this view of him was distorted.

There were several men in plain clothes who

didn't look like the police. The press? White's tongue darted out and ran along his lips.

Further away were the people from Webb Street; there was even a woman with a baby in her arms.

They looked so helpless down there.

A car turned into the road. White could see but not hear it. He dropped the curtain and turned round. Boy was a big silhouette against the landing light, and Barbara saw him and the thing in his hand, the elongated shadow that it threw on the floor.

"Got it?"

"Sure."

"Okay; put the light on. Wait two minutes. A car's just coming along the street; we might hear the bang in a minute. Stand by the head of the stairs."

They moved out of the room. Only their shadows were visible, pale against the brighter light of the room itself. Barbara tried to get up again, and the left elbow let her down. She must have damaged it badly, for pain shot excruciatingly through her arm when she put her weight on it.

She turned onto her other side and tried to get up that way, but her back felt as if it were breaking. She had to clench her teeth against the pain, but suddenly, surprisingly, reached her knees. Her dread seemed like a shrieking demon. She swayed there, fifteen feet from the window—a mile away from the window.

Any moment, she expected the roar of an explosion.

It didn't come.

"They're not here yet," said Boy. "If they don't come—"

"They'll come; the Blower knows what's good for him. We just need time." White glanced at Barbara and pointed. "Go and get busy with her." He went to the microphone and switched it on.

"*West,*" he said, and in the room his voice sounded quiet and controlled, "*I'm going to get busy on those ears. Perhaps that will make you understand that I mean what I say—free passage for all of us, or that will be only the beginning.*"

Barbara tried to get to her feet. She was swaying, as if drunk. Boy, razor in hand, stepped nearer. Whether it was the terror in her eyes, whether it was just an instinct of decency or of pity, she didn't know. He stopped, staring at her.

"Get a move on!" White rasped.

He had forgotten that the loud-speaker was still live. "Here, let me do it, if you're too squeamish. I—"

"*No!*" screamed Barbara, "*no, no!*"

She was near the live microphone.

Outside, the terror in her voice clutched at the hearts and minds of men and women.

Outside, the firemen had almost finished their feverish build-up, hoses were ready, and when they were in position would smash against every window in the flat. The brigade chief came hurrying, hand raised and waving, as the last of those three awful "no's" came from the loud-speaker and blanched tense faces.

"Now!" roared the brigade chief.

"Come on!" Roger shouted.

He led a party of a dozen men toward the garage, and, as he leaped into the road, the water gushed out of the hoses and smashed at the window. Two windows broke. The water sent curtains and blinds billowing, hissed and roared. Some firemen ran an escape up to the windows at the front.

Roger scrambled to the top of a ladder against the main front window; the window that mattered, although he didn't know it. Water sprayed down on him, drenching his head and shoulders. He crouched, waiting for the flood to cease, hearing it roaring inside the room, straining his ears to catch other sounds but hearing only the furious hiss of the hurtling water.

It stopped.

He was on the move in an instant. A great hole gaped in the glass. He smashed several big splinters out, then climbed through. The electric light was still on, the lamp swaying wildly.

Barbara Denny was on the floor in a corner, lying on her stomach, trying to raise herself on her arms, but her left arm sagged. She was drenched. Her eyes looked huge; she was mouthing words which made only a gibberish.

The room was flooded, papers and books, glasses and cloths were floating, and she lay in a pool of water.

Other men came in.

"She's okay," Roger shouted, "look after her!" He heard fighting in other rooms and on the stairs, rushed toward the door, and heard a shot.

Then a cry from the woman stopped him. It was as if a physical barrier were flung in front of him as she cried:

"They're going to blow you up!"

18

The Explosion

Downstairs, scuffling and banging were still going on, but there was no more shooting. Men climbed in at the window; one of them walked halfway toward Barbara. Roger, turning on his heel, saw that she was glaring at him, and he was sure that she knew what she was saying.

He said, "Here? The house?"

"No, no, a car, in the street. It's coming!"

He couldn't hear a car, but he could guess what she meant. This was the Gelignite Gang; they would know how to handle all kinds of explosives. There was all the evidence the police could ever need that the gang had been smoked out of its security, and it was fighting with everything it had.

And he knew what a car loaded with explosives could do.

He ran to the window.

A man was coming up the ladder.

"Get down," he shouted, "get down!" He stared toward the corner of the street and saw a car moving slowly, a long way behind other cars, its head-lamps shining. He heard its engine. He saw it move forward.

Below, the firemen were still at their hoses.

He swung round and grabbed the microphone, shouted into it, and heard the booming of his own voice; thank God it was still live. He fought to speak calmly; shouting would only distort his voice. "Sopley!" he called, "that car at the end of the street is loaded with high explosives. Turn the hoses on it, stop it somehow."

Had Sopley heard?

There were seconds of awful uncertainty when everyone in sight below seemed to stand as still as statues. In the sudden quiet, the engine of the car sounded very loud, had the menacing roar of a buzz bomb. Then people swayed in panic, and began rushing back toward the houses for protection. Two powerful jets of water roared out from the leveled nozzles.

The two jets converged on the windshield of the approaching car.

It was smothered with foamy water, and Roger actually lost sight of it for a moment. Then he saw a man leap from it, fall, pick himself up, and go running toward the end of the street. Next moment, the car loomed out of the sheet of water. It was skidding, and now broadside to Roger. It mounted the curb and crashed against the wall of a house.

A sheet of flame blinded everyone near.

Roger staggered from the window as he heard the roar.

*   *   *

180

It was quiet in the flat and in the street. There was a hush everywhere as awed people, reprieved from danger but not yet released from its spell, stared at the gaping holes in the walls of two houses, the bedding hanging from drooping floors, furniture drooping half in and half out of the houses.

Two men, and White, were prisoners now.

Roger was on his knees beside Barbara Denny. He had helped her lie down, found a cushion for her head, held her hands very tightly, looked down into her terror-haunted eyes.

"It's all over, and you saved them," he said. "It's all over. We'll have you away from here in a few minutes, and you'll be fine."

She began to shiver.

Soon the ambulance men came for her, and, when they had gone, Sopley came with a whisky flask.

"I need that," Roger muttered, and drank neat whisky. "Thanks."

That was at two o'clock.

It was half-past five, quite dark on a lovely, star-lit morning. Only a whispering breeze stole among the trees, only a few leaves loosened from their summer's anchorage and floating into the streets of Chelsea, into the gardens of the houses at Bell Street.

Roger was sitting next to a night-duty sergeant who had driven him here; he had left the new Wol-seley at the Yard. His clothes were soaked, and he was almost stupid with tiredness and whisky fumes, but thoughts were drifting through his mind; over and over again the same thoughts. He was trying to make sure that nothing had been forgotten.

The car approached his Bell Street house and slowed down.

Barbara Denny was in the hospital with a dislocated elbow and bruised back, but no bones broken; she was calmer now. The only really useful thing she'd been able to add was that name—the Blower. White and Boy had telephoned a man they called the Blower, and the Blower had sent the killer car.

Look for the Blower.

The car, a newish Standard, was wrecked, but was known to have false number plates. All Divisions had been alerted to report movements of new Standards that night. They might get a line from that.

The man called Boy was dead; he'd jumped out of a window at the flat and broken his neck. The other two men who had been held with White kept sullenly silent and loyal to their leader, as men like them so often did. Each had a high muscular and a low intelligence rating.

White was the owner of the garage.

All three were now at the Yard, soon to be questioned again.

White had just stood or sat without saying a word, a half grin on his thin, bloodless face.

Some men were born bad, remember.

The police car stopped.

"Here you are, sir," said the sergeant. "I'll nip out and open your door for you, if you like."

"Eh? Oh, no, I'll open it." Roger started to get

182

out. His legs weren't very steady. The sergeant was round at his door and opening it before he had really collected himself. "Thanks." He stepped out.

Brrh, it was cold.

His head reeled.

"Let me have your keys, sir."

"No, I can manage. You get off, plenty to do. I'm shafely home. I—"

His tongue wouldn't behave itself.

The light went on in the hall, then the door opened, and Janet was there, with a dressing gown hugged tightly to her.

"Shee," Roger said, proudly. "My wife's like me, always on duty."

"Oh, it's all right, now Mrs. West is here, sir. Morning, Mrs. West. Nothing to worry about; he—er—he had a bang over the head which knocked him a bit silly, but he's quite all right. Shall I help you in with him?"

"Oh, no, thank you," Janet said. She slid an arm round Roger's waist, felt him lurch against her, smelled the unmistakable and very strong smell of whisky. She didn't say a word about wet clothes. "Do you mean he's *drunk?*"

"Oh, no, ma'am, only had a stiffener or two to keep himself awake. Now he's all in. Maybe the whisky helped to keep him going, that's all." The sergeant—Keen, who had first told Roger about the Jefferson burglary—smiled knowingly at Janet. "Honest, Mrs. West."

"I don't care whether he's drunk or sober, he's home," Janet said. "I can manage, really. If you'll just hold the door open."

Soon she was indoors. Roger straightened up, looked at her, grinned a little foolishly, and

183

winked. "S'all right," he said. "Sober as a judge. Night of triumph. Nearly earned the George Medal I should shink. Think. Night, Keen." His voice changed. "Oh, Keen!"

He stiffened and turned round, although Janet tried to stop him.

"Yes, sir?"

"Very important. All that stush—all that *stuff* beneath White's garage. Jewels, plate, every damned thing. Every single blankety thing must be checked for prints. The *Fingerprints* boys will croak like bullfrogs, but never mind. They're to test every case, every item of shewelry, every—single—blessed—shing! Tell Turnbull." He stopped, gulped, grinned. "That's right, tell Turnbull, he's the man who never needs any shut-eye. And he'll see it's done, too. *Everyshing.* And at the garage. And that Packard. Oh, and was White a customer at Pretzel's?"

"Don't worry, sir, it'll all be done."

"M'boy," said Roger, solemnly, "if you'd worked at the Yard as long as I have, you'd know that there's one way to do a shob—job—ish to do it yourshelf. But my wife won't let me." He shot a wicked smile at Janet. "Next best thing, tell Turnbull, and don't you go home until it's started."

"I'll see it right through, sir."

"Liar," said Roger. "Goo'night." He nodded, grabbed Janet, then straightened up. Her arm was steady and her body sturdy, and unexpectedly she was smiling, not annoyed any more.

They reached the foot of the stairs.

At the head, looking down with wide-eyed gravity, were the boys, Richard clutching Scoopy's arm.

*　　*　　*

Roger stood squarely in front of the bathroom mirror, just after twelve o'clock next morning, and determinedly shaved, each stroke firm and deliberate. He used a safety razor and lather, but kept seeing a big bone-handled cutthroat razor in his mind's eye. That was the thing that affected him most, and it needn't, now. When she had fully recovered, Barbara Denny would be able to put the haunting effect of that out of her mind; she had the right kind of temperament, the right mental balance.

Hadn't she?

He finished shaving, had a quick shower, and went back into the bedroom, naked as the day he was born. Every morning newspaper was in the bedroom—three spread out on the bed, two on the dressing table, one on a chair, others on the floor. They were late editions, and they all had front-page spreads of the night's sensations. He and Barbara Denny provided the illustrations; he'd won with seven pictures to Barbara's six. There were flash-bulb photographs of the wrecked houses and the car, of the garage, and, of course, of Nicholas White being taken out, under arrest and hiding his face.

No newspaper questioned the name—White.

The stories didn't much matter; the general tone of them did. This was a day for great rejoicing at the Yard; Lassitter might almost have prayed for such a moment. For most of the loot from Jefferson's, and some of the loot from the other night raids, had been found at the garage. In a small cellar, the existence of which had not even been suspected by the police, all the machinery of a manufacturing jeweler had been installed; there, trade-marks had been obliterated and others put in their place. Little crucibles and a small electric oven had been found, filled with solid gold; the gold had been melted down from the settings of the stolen jewelry, and new settings were in process of manufacture. Diamonds, rubies, emeralds, and sapphires were neatly hidden behind loose bricks. It was the biggest haul of its kind for years. Every newspaper splashed it on the front page. Even the *Times* had given it a tiny space in the top right-hand corner, usually reserved for epochal events.

Roger saw a stop-press he hadn't noticed before, and bent down to read it.

P.C. Bigglesworth, see page 1, likely to be discharged from Middlesex Hospital today. E.T.

Roger felt a draft; the door opened; Janet stopped on the threshold and said, "Oh!"

He turned round. "Sorry, sweet, but shocked at your time of life?"

"Oh, you fool, they can see right in front across the road, and everyone's looking."

"Nonsense, I'm well back from the window." Roger retreated and picked up his underpants from the chair. "You look wonderful. How do I look?"

"Decadent," declared Janet. "You're getting a pot belly, and—"

"That's a foul slander!"

"—and you have purple rings under your eyes and lines of dissipation at your nose and mouth." She drew nearer.

"Oh, I knew about those," he said, and kissed her. "Was I very bad last night?"

"I've never seen you worse."

"Oh, well," Roger said, suddenly lugubrious. "I suppose you had to find it out later; I've been secretly drinking for years."

"*I* know about that. When you're so flogged out that you can't carry on for another minute, you start tippling whisky to keep you going until you either drop in your tracks or bend at the knees. The boys," she added, straining away from him, "were considerably shocked."

"Oh, no!"

Something in his expression of distress made her laugh. She relaxed and hugged him.

"No, you fool. Anyhow, I told them you were punch drunk. Scoopy knows all about that, but if he looks like taking up boxing seriously *I'm* going to stop him. I don't care at all what you say. That man, Keen, stayed behind and gave them a quick pen picture of what had happened, without any nasty details. So you're still a hero to your own children."

"Bless you, heroine!"

"I was going to bring your lunch up here; I hoped it would make you lie in a bit longer, but it's like dealing with a robot," Janet said. "It's all ready. I know you're famished, and we'll start the minute the boys get in." She sat on the edge of the bed, watching him dress. "This is almost the only chance I get of having a word with you, darling, but must you always be dressing or undressing?"

Roger kept a straight face. "For you, yes."

She stared, momentarily puzzled, and then burst out laughing. "I really believe you get younger!" she said. "You certainly act the fool more than ever you did." She watched him light a cigarette, holding the matches very carefully in his left hand. "How're the fingers?"

"Much better."

"I'll want to see them before I believe you. Let me." She got up, then added searchingly: "Roger, did everything go as well as the newspapers say it did, last night? Are you satisfied?"

"Satisfied?" He submitted to the firm, competent touch of her hands, and looked at her thick dark hair, with those strands of gray, and her small, delicate ear, faintly pink. A cutthroat razor hovered in front of his mind's eye; then Barbara's face, then her scream of warning, then the smashed cars and the gushing water. "No," he said, quietly. "We know that one of the big shots in this is called the Blower, and we think that he's the master of ceremonies during the raids. We know we've got rid of several of the gang, but don't know how many are left. The Blower himself, and who?"

Janet said, "It could be worse, I suppose." She held up his hand and looked at the bruised and grazed fingers in the searching daylight near the window. "I think you ought to bathe them again, and put on some Dettol. They look healthy enough, though." She paused, and looked at him steadily. "Have you any idea who it is?"

"The Blower?"

"Yes, and anyone else you haven't found?"

"Not for certain," Roger said. "Just vague ideas. They may have picked something up at the Yard while I've been sleeping. How many times have they called up for me?"

Janet was surprised into telling the truth. "Six

or seven. They—well, I said you'd call them when you came round! I said I didn't think you'd be well enough to go in today, and unless you're a bigger fool than I think, you won't."

Her voice was almost shrill.

"I am a bigger fool," Roger said firmly. "As you well know. I can see 'Conference' written up in letters of flaming red for this afternoon. But I'll have lunch first!" He cocked his ears, hearing voices outside followed by running footsteps. Suddenly Richard's chuckling laugh came. Richard always laughed as if the joke was the funniest that had ever been made and earned the deepest laughter. Scoopy would grin or give a little chuckle; he didn't surrender to mirth so completely.

"It's nice to know they'll own me this morning." Roger was already at the window, looking out, but the boys were tussling with each other and not looking up. A little crowd of sightseers and several neighbors were. "Fish wriggles like an eel," Roger said. "Scoop—"

"Since you are going to deign to be in to lunch," Janet said, "you might try to reason with your elder son."

'What's he up to now?" Roger asked, then burst out chuckling. "Look! He could break Richard in two, but he's as gentle as a mother hen! Look at the little beggar, holding Richard against the fence and pretending to punch his nose. He plays the fool well enough for the stage."

"He won't go on the stage if I can help it. Anyhow, he'll probably be a parson. He feels a call to help boys less fortunate than he is himself."

Roger swung round. "What?"

"It started with your explanation of people who commit crimes, especially those with a poor start in life," Janet told him. "At lunch time yesterday I was given a long, earnest lecture on philosophy— all about doing the proper thing and what a pity it was about less fortunate boys, and could he bring a boy home to tea? So I let him. Oh, was that brat a little villain! I didn't blame him for being a bit smelly, for needing a haircut or for having a filthy handkerchief, but he was as insolent as they can be—except when Martin was with him. Then he acted like an angel. He sees he's on a good thing in old Scoop. You'll have to cope," Janet added. "He'll certainly start on you—I think he's going to say that this boy only gets sixpence a week pocket money, and couldn't you help out a bit."

"Oh, *is* he?"

"Darling," said Janet, sweetly, "you put the beautiful thoughts into his head; don't fail to practice what you preach or you really will come off your pedestal."

"I'll have to think this one out," Roger said slowly. "I'll temporize this lunch time, pleading haste, and promise to go into it later."

"Coward," said Janet.

Martin, who seemed gifted with a sixth sense about when to force an issue and when to let it wait, raised the subject of his protégé tentatively, and then launched into a long rigmarole about football, silly little girls, and Richard being greedy—which started a long, bitter argument— and if it were fine on Saturday afternoon, could Roger take them to see Fulham? They'd been to

190

Chelsea lately but hadn't seen football at Craven Cottage for weeks.

Roger was promising, conditionally, when the telephone bell rang.

It was Turnbull.

"There's a full-dress conference at two thirty," the sergeant said. "Even I've been dragged in. Sopley, too, and I'm told that Lassitter's coming. We've found out that Dillon worked from White's garage, all the distributing and covering was done from there, and we think we've got a bead on that philandering son of Sarkey's. Thought you'd like to know about this. Chatworth seemed more impressed than I was when your wife said you were only half conscious."

Roger said, "She ought to be used to that by now. Where are you?"

"At the Yard."

"White talked?"

"None of them has."

"I'll be there in about half an hour," Roger said. "How are things at Brickett Street. Anything turned up about the man who shot O'Leary?"

"Not unless it was Boy," said Turnbull. "You'd better come and go through all the reports. Things happen so fast we keep falling behind. The phone call Philip Sarkey had is still a mystery. We don't know why they kidnaped Barbara. Can't understand why they killed O'Leary, either, can you?"

"Sure he worked for them?"

"Oh, yes. He was a manufacturing jeweler, and managed the workshop at the garage. We learned that from the other pair. All we really want is the Blower, though."

"We aren't going to get the Blower without a big

load of trouble," Roger said ominously. "Ask Sopley to guard Rosie and Mulcaster as if they were worth their weight in jewels."

Turnbull sounded startled. "All right, but why?"

"And check if White's a customer at Pretzel's."

"I jumped that gun. He is—goes occasionally. Hick usually has a chat with him."

"Also, watch Hick," Roger urged. "Anything in from that man Marino, the one we planted at Pretzel's?"

"Only oddments," Turnbull said. "Nothing to work on."

"It'll come soon. I'll be seeing you," said Roger, and rang off.

19

Son?

The conference was a flop. Everyone was anxious to be nice and friendly, everyone was feeling replete with results. There had not been time to digest all the evidence. New facts were still coming in. Chatworth seemed to sense this futility early on, but nearly everyone wanted to talk. The only two who said practically nothing were Lassitter and Roger. They sat next to each other, and judging from Lassitter's expression from time to time, Roger felt that they might have more in common than he'd thought before.

Interest quickened when Chatworth turned to Roger and said:

"Why are you so worried about the Mulcasters?"

"I've always believed that Maitland told someone what part of the store he'd be in at a certain time, and that the raid at Jefferson's was made according to known night-watch schedules," Roger said flatly. "If Maitland's suspicions hadn't been aroused—and we know he went downstairs—we probably wouldn't have heard anything until next morning. As it was, we got a start."

Everyone was watching him; Chatworth hopefully.

"Then we know that Mulcaster was hostile from the beginning—scared but hostile. O'Leary seemed to frighten the wits out of him and his wife. Did Mulcaster kill O'Leary, I wonder?"

Chatworth said, almost testily:

"When O'Leary was killed, Mulcaster only just escaped with his life. Doubt the evidence?"

"Yes," Roger said. "Mulcaster might have faked a third party's presence."

"Guesswork," Chatworth grunted. "Why should they turn on each other?"

Roger thought it best to keep quiet.

Beckwith said, "When thieves fall out."

Someone had to say it, and Beckwith looked impatient as he did so. He had dealt with his part of the inquiry by reporting that nitroglycerine, not gelignite, had been used in Webb Street. There was evidence to show that the Standard car had been in position where it could turn round in the road in the shortest possible time. There was little doubt that the driver had planned to come as near as he could get, then hurl the nitroglycerine—packed so that it would explode on sharp contact —and then swing round, mount the pavement, and drive off the way he had come. The jolt when the car had been swung out of the road and into the wall of the house had caused the explosion.

The driver had escaped.

"What's your next move?" Chatworth asked Roger.

"Apart from questioning the prisoners, find out why Miss Denny was kidnaped," Roger said.

No one commented.

The report from the hospital about Barbara was on Chatworth's desk. She hadn't suffered any serious injury; her elbow would soon mend, although she would have to carry her arm in a sling for a while. She had made a statement which cleared up one puzzle: how she had been kidnaped.

She'd gone to her car, aware that men were watching her, and found a tire flat. She'd driven to the nearest telephone, bumping along, knowing that men followed. There had been just time to call Sarkey's flat.

Asked why she hadn't called the police, she had said:

"It was the first number I thought of. I was so frightened."

"I could make a suggestion," Turnbull volunteered.

"Let's hear it." Chatworth hadn't much love for the detective sergeant, but personal dislike didn't affect his judgment.

"Philip Sarkey is extremely wealthy," Turnbull said carefully. "His father is many times a millionaire. The men organizing the series of crimes saw that we had them on the run. If they snatched Miss Denny, they could hold her to ransom. The phone message to Philip Sarkey makes that an obvious possibility—the usual 'lay off the police' angle." Turnbull kept his voice matter-of-fact. "If it hadn't been for the discovery in Webb Street, I think young Sarkey would have had a second demand by now."

He stopped.

"That's a guess, at most," Superintendent Cortland growled.

"There was a call," Turnbull murmured. "And there's evidence that White's got a good mind. You know—"

He stopped.

"Go on, go on," Chatworth said impatiently.

"We've heard a lot of talk about this Reginald Sarkey, Sir Gerald's other son." Roger felt sure that this was the thing Turnbull really wanted to talk about. "He'd be about White's age, wouldn't he? He was always a bad lot, according to the records. I'd like the Sarkeys to be brought face to face with White, Sir Guy. It might lead to nothing, but, if it worked, we'd be somewhere. We might run into a kind of family feud—and knowing Sir Gerald Sarkey, could we be really surprised?"

Chatworth looked round for comment, especially at Roger. He made none; nor did anyone else. Turnbull wasn't sure whether the silence meant aloofness and disapproval, or whether it was genuine uncertainty.

"That's what I'd try, anyhow," he said flatly.

"Any objection, West?" Chatworth barked.

"Might be a good idea," Roger said mildly, and Turnbull, momentarily hot under the collar, looked at him with unexpected humility, offering a silent "Thanks."

It was nearly five o'clock that afternoon.

Roger stood in a little crowd of women, with two other men, outside a lift at Jefferson's. The ground floor was a seething mass of people; this was a special-offer day. A lift arrived, disgorged another twenty people to join the mob, and absorbed the

196

waiting crowd; Roger was last in. He found himself imagining Barbara Denny here, and wondering again why she had been kidnaped. He hadn't seen her since last night; he wanted to.

Soon, Sarkey's secretary, in a fresh white blouse and the same black skirt, was saying:

"Oh, yes, Sir Gerald is ready to see you."

Sir Gerald Sarkey sat behind his desk, in exactly the same pose as before; Roger studied his pale, thin face for a likeness to White, but there was no actual facial likeness, possibly a faint similarity of expression and of coloring. White had a broader face, a different-shaped chin—there were dozens of points of difference.

Philip Sarkey was no more like his father than he was like White, if it came to that.

"Good evening, Chief Inspector." Sarkey stood up and, to Roger's surprise, shook hands; he had a cold hand, a brief but firm enough grip. "I have to offer you my congratulations. And my thanks."

"I'll pass them on, Sir Gerald, thank you," Roger said. "That was a combined-operations job if ever I've known one!" He shot a quick smile at Philip. "How is Miss Denny?"

"She's doing fine, just fine!" Philip looked ten years younger than he had the previous night. "Everything will be all right now." His grin was almost boyish, and he fluttered an eyelid, obviously intending to tell Roger that there was peace between Barbara and his father.

"What can we do to help you, Chief Inspector?" Sarkey asked, mildly.

"We took several prisoners last night," Roger said, "and we would like both you and Mr. Philip to come and have a look at them. For purposes of

197

identification only, of course. And—" he paused to give the Sarkeys time to comment or protest, but neither did—"and there are two dead men we would like you to look at, too. It's not pleasant, but—"

"If it is necessary, we had better comply," the older man said. His gesture and his expression showed distaste, but he raised no objection. "When do you require this scrutiny to take place?"

"Can you come now, sir?" asked Roger.

They saw one body after the other. The first two were in the morgue attached to the AZ Divisional HQ—the man named Boy and the big-torsoed Day, who had been taken from the car in Tivvy Docks. Neither father nor son showed the slightest sign of recognition. Roger let them catch sight of O'Leary, whose head had been patched up, and whose face seemed hardly touched. They passed him without a second glance.

It was chilly in the morgue.

Roger went with them, in Sarkey's chauffeur-driven Daimler, to Scotland Yard, led them to the lift, led them to his office, along the wide corridors which echoed to the sound of their footsteps. Then he tapped at the door of the Assistant Commissioner's office and, as arranged, opened it and went straight in.

White, standing alone, was facing the door. Chatworth was just behind it.

Sir Gerald Sarkey checked his movement, almost stumbled, recovered himself, and went slowly into the room. Philip, hidden by his father from White for a moment, caught sight of his expression and then stopped.

"I'm sorry to cause you this distress, Sir Gerald," Roger said, while Sarkey looked at him icily and White sneered, "and I was anxious not to cause unnecessary embarrassment; that's why I didn't warn you. If this man were a stranger, it wouldn't have mattered. This *is* your son, Reginald Sarkey, isn't it?"

The older man stood there, silvery hair shimmering under the bright office light, pale face absolutely empty of color, lips little more than a thin line. He stared at Nicholas White, and White looked back at him, thin lips twisted in a sneering smile.

"I have one son alive, named Philip Robin," said Sir Gerald Sarkey evenly. "I lost my elder son, many years ago."

He turned his back on the prisoner, and his gaze had a cutting edge as he looked toward Roger. He didn't speak; yet contempt could not have been more plainly uttered. For the first time, he acknowledged Chatworth, giving a slight nod of the head. Then he went to the door and Philip hurried to open it for him.

"Sir Gerald—" Chatworth began.

Sarkey went out, shoulders squared, back ramrod straight. He did not hurry. Philip hesitated, looked angrily into Roger's eyes, and then turned after his father.

Roger didn't appear to hurry but he caught up with Philip and then with Sarkey, who must have known that he was there but did not turn his head, just walked steadily toward the lift.

"There are two ways of doing this," Roger said. "Admitting it now, and making it easy for us. Or compelling us to prove it by subpoenaing you, forcing you into the witness box at the Old Bailey, having it in banner headlines in the newspapers. You can take your choice. You'll get publicity anyhow, but if it's done the way you seem to want it, it'll hurt ten times as much."

Neither man spoke.

Roger said, "Our job here is to stop crime. We don't always like the way we have to do it. We don't always like the consequences of it. But it's obvious that someone has been gunning for you, as obvious that you think it is your elder son, Sir Gerald. If it isn't, that's too bad."

Philip rasped, "Why the devil don't you leave him alone? Why are you hounding him like this?"

The lift stopped in front of them. The attendant opened the gates. Sir Gerald stepped in, Philip followed him, and the attendant said to Roger:

"You coming, sir?"

"No, thanks," said Roger.

He stood waiting while the lift carried father and son out of sight. Sir Gerald Sarkey actually looked toward him, without expression, as if he were facing a brick wall.

Roger went slowly back to Chatworth's office, and to the man who might be Sarkey's disowned son.

Sarkey had been the victim of those mock attacks. Barbara had been savagely treated. White might be the leader of the gang, but he had telephoned the Blower, whose name implied that he was the expert with high explosives. No nitroglycerine, TNT, or explosive of any kind had been found at the garage, so a store of that was hidden somewhere, and the man who'd used it before might use it again.

Whom would he strike at next?

The next day was a gritty one of work in the Yard, and a bad one outside. Fog turned to smog, thick, and gray-yellow, slowing down traffic and getting on nerves which were already strained. The only good reports to come in were about Barbara Denny; she seemed to have withstood the shock to the mind. Roger didn't try to see the Sarkeys. Nicholas White refused to say a helpful word; he was remanded for eight days at the police-court hearing.

Billy Mulcaster, Hick, and everyone remotely connected with the case behaved quite normally. Roger had every available man working on them, but couldn't find anything to justify holding them.

Rosie was only a ghost of a woman: pallid, husky, silent.

The Sarkeys went to the Oxford Street store as usual. Philip left soon after ten o'clock, and police en route reported that his Rolls-Bentley purred a casual eighty along the road as far as Reading, where Jefferson's had a store. There was another big one-day sale, and Philip behaved as he always did, getting back to the Oxford Street store a little before four o'clock.

Roger was touchy, Turnbull sour, and a mass of routine work kept them anchored to their desks. The fear of another attack, perhaps on the girl, perhaps on Sarkey, possibly on Philip, nagged at Roger's mind. Report after negative report came in.

It was one of those days.

Roger left the office soon after six o'clock, and while he'd known worse fogs, the usual twenty minutes' run home took him nearly forty. He put the car into the garage, a kind of defiant: "I'm not going out again tonight for anyone," and then turned toward the lighted house.

He was a yard away from the front door when it opened with a bang; three shouting, jumping, bouncing boys rushed out. Martin called Scoopy and Richard leaped at him at the same moment, and he held them off with difficulty. The third boy hung back, rather out of place. Martin dropped into a boxing stance, Richard pranced about as if he were a champion wrestler, and Roger fought them off with one arm, protecting his injured hand. Their delight passed itself on to him; when at last he called *"Pax"* he had forgotten the fog, the routine, the day's gloomy reactions, the present impasse.

"That's plenty for tonight, boys, but you'll soon have to let me tackle you one at a time." He glanced at the other lad and recognized Peter Smith, Scoopy's protégé. "Hallo, Peter, how're tricks?"

"All right, Mr. West, thank you. I've got to go home now."

"How far is that?"

"Well, not very far."

"Ooh, it is!" cried Richard, "it's miles and miles!"

"It isn't *very* far," Martin put in. "About one mile, I should think; don't take any notice of Richard, he *always* exaggerates. We were going to walk halfway with Peter, but Mum says we mustn't, because of the fog."

"She's quite right. What's the address, Peter?"

"Mortimer Road, sir, but I shall be all right, I will really."

Mortimer Road was at least two miles away, and no bus from the end of Bell Street went anywhere near it. On a foggy night, it was nearly an hour's walk. Roger hesitated, then said:

"Wait here a minute, chaps, I want a word with your mother." He left them putting their hands in front of their noses and pretending that the fog made the fingers invisible; then Martin called Scoopy, with his gift of playing the fool, started imagining things that weren't there. Horses, rockets, space ships, cowboys...

Janet was in the kitchen, ironing, with the radio on low.

"Hallo, darling." Roger slid his arms round her and kissed the nape of her neck. "Anything good for supper?"

"Yes, as usual! But it won't be ready for half an hour. Finished for the day?" She was hopeful.

"The real work. This Smith child is a long way from home, though. I think I ought to get the car out again and take him. I *would* choose to put the damned thing away tonight! Shall I take the boys?"

"If you like, but—" Janet stood the iron upright on its stand and turned to look at him—"be careful, the fog's getting worse."

"I've known it twice as thick. How's the protégé doing?"

"You know," said Janet, thoughtfully, "I think I like him better than I did. If I'd followed my nose the first time I'd have told Scoopy not to bring him again, but now—well, he had a bath last night, for one thing! And he was telling me about his mother and father. Quite soberly, you know how children do. The father gets drunk most weekends, and straps him, the mother just sits and cries her eyes out. Obviously she spoils the child, the father is much too harsh, and—oh, well, it's none of my business. But you might ask the policemen round Mortimer Road to keep their eyes and ears open."

"I will," promised Roger.

He went out and told the boys about the car jaunt. Richard whooped with delight, Martin rushed to help open the garage doors, and young Peter Smith just looked up at Roger, wide-eyed in the foggy gloom.

When they dropped him outside his house he muttered a hushed thanks.

"I hope his father doesn't spank him tonight," Martin said. "He uses a strap with a buckle. I don't think it's fair, do you, Dad?"

"Different people, different ideas," said Roger. "And keep your feet off the backs of those seats, you lump. How's school been today?"

"Ooh, Dad, I got twenty out of twenty for English, wasn't that good?" cried Richard. "It's better than Martin, even...."

It was a soothing, oddly restful evening.

The fog didn't lift.

"It looks as if the worst might be over," Chatworth said to Roger about ten o'clock next morning. "If White's the killer and Sarkey's son, we know the motive for making Sarkey's life hell. I didn't ever think I'd feel sorry for Sir Gerald Sarkey, but I do." As always, Chatworth could be bluffly human. "But we're still in a hurry. We want the man who ran away from the Standard car just before it crashed—and we want whoever sent him with that explosive. How did he get away?"

"Two Divisional chaps on duty at the corner of Webb Street swear that the Standard had a press label stuck on the windshield," Roger said. "There was only the driver, with his hat pulled well down. The explosion surprised them; they were still reeling when he staggered past. I've checked at Pretzel's. Hick had a telephone call about the time Boy called the Blower from the garage. Billy Mulcaster was on late duty, and left about two—just time to have got to Webb Street so as to blow the car up. Our chap, Marino, stuck to Hick, who went to his flat near Shepherd's Market, and a Central Division man followed Billy Mulcaster. Billy slipped him, and got home half an hour after the explosion."

"So he could be the Standard's driver. Questioned him? Were his clothes wet?"

"He wouldn't necessarily get wet," Roger said. "He wasn't, anyway. I'd like to let him think he's in the clear on this job, anyhow. I'd also like to make Sir Gerald Sarkey talk. If White's his son, we've got a motive. If he isn't—"

"You'll never get a word out of Sarkey," Chatworth prophesied.

"We can try." Roger was almost brusque. "I'll go and see him. If I can make him believe there's danger for himself and Barbara, he might see sense."

It was Sir Gerald Sarkey's invariable custom to be at his desk at nine thirty on the few occasions when he stayed in London—he had, that night, at a hotel. He was always driven to Jefferson's side entrance by his chauffeur, and usually the car came back for him at about eleven. A Yard sergeant was watching from the corner of Oxford Street next morning. A yellow pall hung at rooftop height, and although visibility wasn't really bad, traffic moved slowly and cautiously. There wasn't a breath of wind.

The sergeant saw Sarkey arrive, and went off to telephone the Yard and West.

Sarkey, meanwhile, went up to his office as if nothing had happened, was his usual aloof but polite self to his secretary, whose white blouse seemed very white and whose black skirt was beautifully pleated.

He sat at his desk, took out his keys, pushed one into the top left-hand drawer—by which his secretary was standing.

The telephone bell rang.

"All right, I'll answer it," said Sarkey, and leaned toward the telephone, on the right-hand side of the desk. "Open the drawer and get my things out, Miss Wellesley, will you?"

"Yes, sir."

"Yes, what is it?" Sarkey asked, into the mouthpiece.

"It's Mr. West of the Yard, sir, asking to speak to you."

Sarkey drew in a sharp breath, a veritable hiss of annoyance, and started to move his head back, taking the telephone from his ear. His secretary pulled open the drawer. As she did so, there was a vivid flash, a muffled roar, and an ear-splitting scream; three in one. Then Sarkey felt the blast of the explosion; he dropped the telephone and fell sideways from his chair.

His secretary had collapsed over the desk, and lay quite still.

Her snow-white blouse was sprayed with crimson.

20

Yet More to Come?

Roger West, a police surgeon and three men from the Yard swung into Sir Gerald Sarkey's office just fifteen minutes later. Nothing had been touched. Sarkey himself was standing up, his face absolutely colorless and his eyes peculiarly bright and glittering. Philip was with him, as well as two senior executives of Jefferson's and the staff doctor. Two uniformed policemen stood by the body of the secretary, one on either side. She had fallen from the desk and now lay in a heap on one side. The front of her blouse was crimson with her own blood.

The staff doctor said, "There wasn't a thing we could do. It just made a shambles of her face."

Roger looked down stonily.

"Can't we cover that up?" Philip demanded. His voice was higher pitched than usual.

"Very soon," Roger said. His men were already fixing the tripod for the cameras. "Be as quick as you can. Photographs, diagrams, prints, especially prints." He moved to Philip. "Were you here when it happened?"

"No, I was coming out of the lift. I heard the explosion and—"

"Right, thanks. Will you weigh in right now, finding out who had access to the office? Night watchmen, cleaners, clerical staff, anyone who might have come in here after Sir Gerald left last night. Every minute might help," Roger added brusquely. "I've already sent a car to night watchman Archer's home; you needn't put him on your list."

Philip drew in his breath, looked as if he were going to argue, then glanced at his father, relaxed, and muttered:

"All right."

"Thanks." Roger didn't glance across as Philip hurried out. "Exactly what happened, Sir Gerald?" He was crisp and matter-of-fact, as if oblivious of or indifferent to the body on the floor.

A light flashed; there was a sharp sound as the photographer's lamp flared. It gave the room an uncanny light, turned Sir Gerald Sarkey's pallor to an unnatural, sickly whiteness, and shimmered on his glittering eyes.

But the chairman of Jefferson's told Roger exactly what had happened in a flat, emotionless voice.

"I see, sir," Roger said, and paused while a plain-clothes man finished putting down shorthand notes of the statement. "You understand, naturally, that this was an attempt on your life, and that because you were leaning toward the telephone when the explosion came, your secretary was killed instead of you."

"I am fully aware of it," Sarkey said. "I am equally aware that it was your telephone call which saved my life. And cost Miss Wellesley hers."

"Did you expect an attack on your life?"

"Had I expected that attack I would have taken precautions."

Roger said, "Yes, and if you'd told me the truth last night, you might have stopped this happening. Let's finish arguing, and get at some facts. Was the man you saw last night your elder son?"

Sarkey looked as if he hated him.

"No," he said. "He was a friend of Reginald, that is all."

Roger didn't intend to stay long, but while he was there he looked about for any trifle which might give him the line he so badly wanted. Some papers placed untidily on Sir Gerald's desk had obviously been blown out of the drawer by the explosion.

It would not be so easy to look through these again, and he took the chance.

Only one was of hopeful interest: a letter for Morgan's, a small private inquiry agency.

Roger left the office and went downstairs. The huge ground floor was a seething mass of people, all vivid in the bright fluorescent lighting. Yellow mist was everywhere, and outside the fog was much thicker.

Roger went straight to Morgan's. He knew Pop Morgan, a little, twinkling man, who didn't try to evade the question.

"You'd get this out of me sooner or later, anyway," he said. "Sarkey's had me looking for Reginald, his eldest son. I'm pretty sure it's Hick, the chef at Pretzel's. Know Pretzel's?"

"Yes," Roger said, softly. "I know Hick, too."

"They pay you coppers too well these days!" Morgan grinned, his plump red cheeks almost hiding his gray eyes. "I told Sarkey, and also told him that, according to a friend of Hick, a crook named O'Leary, Hick also had a son."

"Do you know the son?" Roger demanded.

"Name of Mulcaster. Billy Mulcaster's the old boy's grandson, at that rate."

Roger actually winced.

"Got a pain?" asked Morgan.

"Any proof that Mulcaster is Hick's son?"

"Just O'Leary's word—and the knowledge that Mulcaster works at Pretzel's and gets plenty of favors from Hick. But that's a long way from proof."

"Why would anyone invent a grandson for Sarkey if there wasn't one?" asked Roger.

"That's your problem," Morgan said. "I turned in my report, spent half an hour answering Sarkey's questions as if I was being grilled by the original Inquisitors, and then was shown the door. But he paid all right, and the note he sent with his check couldn't have been friendlier. It even made me wonder," Morgan went on slowly, "whether Sarkey's the cold fish he makes out."

Roger said: "We get the same ideas. Thanks, Pop."

Two hours later, Roger went into his office. He had turned the inquiry agent's story over in his mind, without reaching any conclusion. Mulcaster might be Sarkey's grandson, or it might be a smoke screen. If Hick was the disowned son, he might hope that his father would relent toward a grandson—that would make a grandson a good possible investment, would perhaps explain it if Hick was inventing a son.

There was no more news about Hick's past. He had appeared in London several years ago; no one knew from where. The policeman now working as a waiter at Pretzel's had sent a perfect set of Hick's fingerprints to the Yard; Hick hadn't a record.

Roger went into the office, and Turnbull rushed toward him, not just throwing his weight about but genuinely excited; Turnbull's terrific enthusiasm was one of the things that made him bearable.

"Night watchman Archer's downstairs," he rasped. "He knows a thing or two, and I think he'll crack if you go for him hard enough. I took him halfway, and thought he'd better have time to stew."

Roger said sharply, "Sure?"

"Damned nearly."

"All right, thanks," Roger said, "we'll go and see him." He turned to the sergeant who had been with him at Jefferson's. "Get your notes transcribed as soon as you've put out the instructions I gave you in the car."

"Yes, sir."

"Come on," Roger said to Turnbull. "Waiting room?"

Turnbull nodded.

"There's alarm and despondency over at Jefferson's," Roger went on. "An attack on the great Sir Gerald himself really meant something. I made an interesting discovery." They were hurrying to the stairs.

"What's that?"

"A lot of them there *like* the cold fish."

"That's okay," said Turnbull, "the Dinkas of the Nile have a love life, too." He was just ahead of Roger as they went down the stairs to the next floor. "Get anything from him?"

"White isn't his son."

"Sure?"

"He said—" Roger began, and then missed a step. "I see what you mean. Would he deny it, simply to help to keep the name of Sarkey unblemished?" He pondered. "I don't think so, not this time. He'd been very close to death, and he knows as well as I do that whoever tried today will probably try again tomorrow. I think he told me the truth, and I think he'll help as much as he can now. I've a list of other people who had access to his office—it's fantastic but true that a lot of people could have done this. Five clerks who worked late last night, four cleaners who always work on that floor, two night watchmen, including Archer."

"It was Archer," Turnbull said flatly. "Wouldn't I like to be able to knock a confession out of him! I'd make him sweat."

"You always were a moron," Roger said.

He opened the door of the waiting room. A uniformed sergeant stood inside, and night watchman Archer jumped up from an upright chair. He forgot his black bowler and it fell down and clattered on the floor, the brim taking the brunt of the fall. He didn't seem to notice that. He wore a thick Melton topcoat over his neatly pressed navy blue suit, and his face was almost as pale as Sir Gerald Sarkey's.

He looked at Turnbull, obviously scared.

Roger was taking out his cigarettes. He held out

the packet. Archer glanced down, then looked into Roger's eyes, astonished at the proffered friendliness. He took a cigarette and accepted a light; his fingers were trembling, his lips weren't steady.

"You know, Archer," Roger said, "if you do a thing you shouldn't under pressure, it isn't necessarily held against you. And there's such a thing as Queen's evidence. After our last chat, I came to the conclusion that you weren't a bad chap but wondered if you'd got yourself into a nasty jam. If you have, we may be able to help you out of it."

Turnbull was actually looking away from Archer to hide his ludicrous expression of dismay.

Archer grabbed Roger's arms.

"I don't know what's happened now, Mr. West, but I didn't mean any harm last night, any more than I did when I tried to keep Jem Maitland on the top floors. If he'd done what I said he'd be alive now, you can't deny that. I knew there was going to be a raid, I—I lifted a few quid from my last job, that's why I was sacked from it, Mr. West, and these swine discovered about it. Got me to tell them all about the timing on night duty, then checked with Maitland to check me. I daren't lie, I tell you! They worked on me, worked me to death. I got a sick wife, and couldn't afford to be out of a job. I—I know I shouldn't have done it, but I hadn't the guts to stand up against them, that's— that's the sober truth. And the same thing last night. I don't know the guy who worked on me about that, but—but he put on the squeeze. Just told me to put a little packet in Sarkey's desk, said it would scare the wits out of him. I've done that twice before, when I've been told to." The torrent of words was stemmed for a moment; Archer's fingers were tight round Roger's forearm. "What's happened, Mr. West? That sergeant's scared me stiff. Sarkey ain't dead, is he?"

Roger freed himself, gently.

"Someone died," he said. "It wasn't Sarkey."

Archer backed away on stumbling feet, face beginning to fold into grotesque lines of dread. Turnbull turned to look at him, and breathed a resigned: "All right, you win." Roger watched the crumpling face, and even felt compassion.

"We'll help you all we can, Archer," he said quietly. "Who are the people who forced you into this?"

"A man—a man named White started it," Archer muttered. "Him and another guy, O'Leary, they've got a garage near my flat. When I heard what had happened to them I—I just dropped down on my knees. I thought I'd be in the clear. Then I got this message about Sarkey's desk. Chap met me in the street, young swine he was, but I didn't see him clearly, I swear that. I could tell he was young. Then—then your chaps came round. Mr. West," Archer went on, and unexpectedly his manner took on a kind of dignity, "I wouldn't have had anything to do with it if I'd known murder would result. I swear I wouldn't. But I just hadn't the guts to refuse to plant that packet in Sarkey's desk. What —what was in it?"

"It might be better for you if you didn't know," Roger said.

A Yard consultant on explosives reported that morning that the explosive had almost certainly been nitroglycerine packed in a water-absorbent tube. The tube was first soaked in water and filled with the explosive. While the container remained swollen, the nitroglycerine could be carried safely —only a violent blow would make it go off. As the tube dried out and the deadly liquid could move about inside it, only a little jolt was needed to make it explode.

Fragments of a tube were found in Webb Street as well as at Sir Gerald Sarkey's office.

Roger was in the A.C.'s office early that afternoon.

"So the attempt on Sir Gerald's life could have been planned before White was taken prisoner," Chatworth said. "White could have passed on the order and the packet."

"Apparently, sir."

"Then we're back at the possibility, or the probability, that the disowned son was White, and that when he saw his game was coming to an end he played his final card. Kill his father, kidnap his brother's girl and hold her to ransom."

"I suppose we *are* back there." Roger sounded reluctant.

"Well, what's your objection?" Chatworth demanded. "If White was after money from Philip Sarkey, he would reason that he'd be more likely to get it if Philip knew that he wouldn't hesitate to kill, wouldn't he?"

"He could also reason that Philip Sarkey might be the type who wouldn't give a damn for physical danger, and be murderous himself if his father were killed," Roger said. "Whether Nicholas White is Sarkey's son or not, and I don't see Sarkey as a liar, we've still got to find the Blower, and the Blower is a killer who'd cheerfully kill and maim dozens of people, as he tried at Webb Street. White and the other prisoners won't talk, and we can't make them. Archer's story ends at the garage, and apart from the Sarkeys there are only two angles we can work on now—Hick and Pretzel's Restaurant, and the Mulcasters. I've just been studying the reports from the men who've been watching them."

Chatworth nodded. He was sitting at his big desk, his big round face mahogany brown, grizzled hair like a halo of crimped wire. There was a haze about the lighted lamps, and the fog pressed thick and yellow at the windows.

"Well, go on."

"We've a detective officer from Hammersmith, named Marino, at Pretzel's," Roger told him. "He was a waiter before he joined the force; just the right man. He's noticed nothing wrong. Hick's still understaffed, and Bill Mulcaster is behaving normally. Marino says he's a good waiter, has the right way with customers, and gets big tips. The other waiters doubt if he puts everything he gets into the *tronc*, but they all do pretty well, and they let it pass. Mulcaster doesn't seem particularly scared. Marino's checked the relationship between Mulcaster and O'Leary. You know that O'Leary did repair jobs on the cutlery and silver plate, don't you? That's why he was so often at the restaurant. He gave Billy Mulcaster plenty of racing tips, and they usually turned up. Sometimes Billy passed them on, and most of the staff made a good thing out of it. That's another reason why no one was too finicky about Billy not putting all his gratuities into the common pool. Billy himself says that on the night of Maitland's murder O'Leary asked him

217

if he could stay at Brickett Street, and he couldn't very well refuse." Roger paused, put a hand to his pocket and touched his cigarettes, let them go again. One didn't smoke in Chatworth's office until Chatworth said the word. "That's plausible, anyway. When I get half a chance I'm going to try to break Mulcaster's stories—the one for Maitland's night, and the one for last night."

"What was it for last night?"

"He went out of Pretzel's for an hour because he had a headache—just strolled round Soho," Roger said.

"What about that wife of his?"

"She's a nervous wreck," Roger said flatly. "Jumps a yard at unexpected noises, hates going out alone. Naturally enough, perhaps. She had some nasty shocks. I've thought of asking Miss Denny to have another go at making her talk. Rosie might, now."

"Think Miss Denny will play?"

"I think she'll do anything to help see this thing through." Roger was emphatic. "Neither she nor Philip Sarkey has any idea that the attempt on Sarkey's life was planned before. White was arrested, so they'll be afraid of more attempts. That might help to loosen their tongues—Miss Denny's particularly. She may be able to help about White too; may be able to tell us for sure whether he's the other son. Philip just won't tell us, but he may have let something out to Miss Denny. I haven't worried her today, but will tomorrow if the doctors will let me. Apart from that, I think everything's been taken as far as we can take it. But I admit I'm as nervous as a kitten."

Chatworth looked at him straightly, then saw his hand at his pocket, and growled:

"Smoke if you want to. What's making you nervous?"

"When O'Leary was killed, and the man Day was found in the car at Tivvy Docks, it began to look as if the G.G. boys were turning against one another. If that's true, which of them might be killed next? And if White isn't Starkey's son, if the Blower is really the man who's laid all this on—seventeen successful raids, the murders, the feud against Sarkey, not forgetting tossing nitroglycerine among that crowd last night—I'll be nervous until we've got him behind bars. Hick, at the Pretzel, is just about the only man on our list. What worries me is that it may be someone we don't know yet."

Chatworth ruminated, and then rumbled, "Well, don't wear yourself out on it. Go home early tonight, not much you can do in a pea souper like this. Take it easy, and when you've slept on it you may get some bright ideas. How're Janet and the boys?"

"Fine, thanks."

"Lucky chap," Chatworth said. "Family to be proud of. All right, that's all, keep me posted."

Roger went straight down to his own office. All the lights were on, and the fog crept and sniffed at the windows. The street lights on the Embankment and Westminster Bridge were only just visible as little patches of misty white. Cars and buses were vague, dark shapes. Noise was muffled. Roger finished his cigarette and turned to the desk. He would telephone Janet and tell her he'd be home for supper. Chatworth was right; there wasn't a thing he could do except let the case nag at him, and that wouldn't help. An hour or two with the boys, a quiet evening with Janet and the television play would help to clear his mind as well as rest him physically. He began to look forward to it.

He actually touched the telephone, when it rang and made him jump. He grinned as he put it to his ear.

"West speaking."

"There's a woman on the line, sir," said the operator. "She wants to speak to you personally. She says it's very important, and she sounds extremely agitated. Will you speak to her?"

"Yes. Did she give a name?"

"She wouldn't," said the operator. "Just a second, sir—" The line went dead. Then: "You're through."

Roger spoke very casually, anxious not to worsen the unknown woman's agitation.

"This is Roger West here."

"Oh, Mr. West," the woman said, and he knew in a flash that it was Rosie Mulcaster. "I'm so frightened, I don't know what to do. Could I—could I meet you somewhere?"

"Why, yes, Rosie, anywhere you like." Rosie glanced up at the dark fog massed against the window. "I'll come to you, and—"

"No, not here! Say—say Charing Cross station." So she'd thought this out. "I can get a tube from Whitechapel to Charing Cross, under—under the bridge, where the barrow boys are. The fog won't matter there." Rosie kept her head, whatever the cause of her fears. "You won't let me down, Mr. West, will you?"

"I'll be waiting for you. But, Rosie, can't you tell me what it's about? That would be quicker—"

"I mustn't stay in the telephone box," Rosie said. "He—I mean, someone might see me, and—and squeal. I got to talk to you about my Billy, Mr. West, don't let me down."

She hung up without another word.

Rosie Mulcaster put down the receiver and turned round in the little square telephone kiosk. This was the one from which Barbara Denny had telephoned. The fog, a still, yellow mass, was like a wall. She could not see even the outline of a street lamp ten yards away.

There was a sound of someone walking slowly.

She pushed open the heavy door; it creaked enough to frighten her. Outside, she let it go and it clanged noisily.

She turned toward the Whitechapel Road and the station, away from Brickett Street and Billy

Now, she was in terror of *her* Billy.

And the fog was much worse. She began to wonder if she would get to the station.

She heard footsteps behind her, and they drew closer. It was no use turning round to see. She tried to hurry—and banged into a mailbox. Then light glowed faintly in the fog; she could see shapes. Her heart pounded as the footsteps grew nearer. She turned, to see the vague outline of a man.

Billy!

Then, he pounced, and his fingers stifled her scream.

21

Poor Rosie

Roger put the receiver down slowly, stared at the blanketed windows for a long moment, then lifted the telephone and asked for AZ Division. Sopley wasn't in, his chief inspector was.

"Oh, sure," the C.I. said in answer to Roger's question, "Rosie Mulcaster's being followed whenever she goes out. Not that she ever goes far. We've got a good man on that job, too."

"Fine. But send another, and see if you can pick her up. She's just been on the telephone, possibly the one near her home. She's going to get a train from Whitechapel station and meet me at Charing Cross. Have a man at the station, anyway, looking out for her."

"If you say so, but what's all this about?"

"Just my nerves," said Roger. "I want to make sure she gets here. It's a filthy night, and I'd hate anything to go wrong. Make it snappy, will you?"

"I've got the other telephone in my hand," the C.I. assured him blandly.

"Thanks," Roger said, and rang off.

Even if Rosie caught a train at once, she couldn't get to Charing Cross in less than half an hour. He had time to kill.

Twenty minutes later he went downstairs and into the yard to get his car. It was like walking into a smoky blanket. He coughed and paused, losing his bearings. He could see nothing in the yard itself, only a hint of light some distance off. So he would be better to walk; perhaps he had left it too long after all.

He couldn't hurry; the fog was too thick. Traffic was crawling, a few cars had already been parked at the curbs and left stranded. Long streams of cars, lorries and buses were almost bumper to bumper. The pavement was thronged with people hurrying to the underground, the one way home that wasn't likely to take much longer than usual.

At Charing Cross, it seemed a little clearer. Roger made out the green haze of a traffic light at the junction of Whitehall Place and Northumberland Avenue, and darted across. A motorcyclist, coming too fast, nearly caught him. He cursed it and the driver swore at him. He reached the other side safely. Under the bridge, the fog was almost opaque, but the newsboys and the barrow boys were calling out; there was a jostling crush of people in the entrance to the station; everyone was trying to go home by tube.

Rosie would be delayed, too, so he wasn't late.

That was at half-past five.

Rosie hadn't arrived at seven o'clock.

Roger telephoned AZ Division twice. The first time, the Senior Inspector was sarcastic; yes, of course his men would look after Rosie. One of them had reported that she was on her way to Whitechapel Road, and he was after her. The second time, his sarcasm had gone. The Senior Inspector had expected further word by then; he had told his men to report regularly. They'd not done so for nearly an hour.

At five past seven, Roger was on the telephone again. The crowd at the station was much thinner, the fog almost impenetrable.

"Found her yet?" He hadn't realized how desperately Rosie's safety mattered.

"Yes, we've found her," the Senior Inspector told him grimly. "My chaps lost her in the fog, after one was clouted over the head. He'll be okay, but whether the doctors can save Rosie's life, I wouldn't like to say.... Eh?...Oh, she was nearly strangled."

"It's a brute of a job," the house surgeon at the hospital told Roger. "You knew she was expecting, didn't you? Well, she's lost the child, although she may live herself. But the look in her eyes—I thought I'd seen everything, but this kid—"

"Can she talk?"

"No. Not yet, anyhow."

"She might have seen the man who nearly strangled her," Roger said, "might have recognized him. If she did, we could have a killer in custody tonight. If it won't do Rosie too much harm, let me have a couple of minutes with her."

The house surgeon said, "Well, all right. Just two minutes."

They'd taken her to a general ward and put a screen round her bed. A policewoman, notebook on her lap, sat at one side of the bed, out of Rosie's line of vision. The house surgeon moved the big screen aside, and Roger rounded it. Rosie looked at him blankly. Her eyes were huge; he had never seen greater pallor; and he knew exactly what the house surgeon meant.

"Hallo, Rosie," he said, moving to her side. "I ought to have come and seen you earlier. Feeling better?"

She stared blankly.

"Did you see who it was?" asked Roger gently. "Was it anyone you recognized, anyone you'd ever seen before?"

Rosie stared.

"It's very important, Rosie," Roger went on. He wasn't sure that she heard him, or, if she heard, whether she understood a word. "It might be the man who killed your father, you know, and who nearly killed Billy. You ought to try—"

"*Oh, go away, go away, go away,*" cried Rosie, piteously. "*Go away!*"

The house surgeon said, "Sorry, Chief Inspector."

"It's all right," Roger responded quietly. "I won't worry her any more." He didn't go at once, but stood looking down at Rosie. A few days ago she had been radiant with the moment's joy and the wonder of the future; now the past, the present, and the future had all been ruthlessly trampled underfoot.

Roger went away.

From a telephone in the night sister's office, he spoke to the Yard.

"Put a general call out for Billy Mulcaster," he ordered. "Have his home watched. Send men to the Pretzel Restaurant. Wherever he's seen, hold him. Be very careful. Understood?"

"Yes, sir. Any charge?"

"Not yet, just bring him in." Roger put down the receiver, looked at the house surgeon without speaking, and found himself lighting a cigarette, with the packet already back in his pocket. He hooked it out again and proffered it. "Sorry. You've been very good. I'm afraid she's got to stay in hell for a bit longer." He turned out of the office and went down the wide stairs, not noticing the clean smell of the antiseptics, the fresh-looking nurses, or the open doors of the wards and the rows of beds. He felt more sure than ever that the man he wanted—or *a* man he wanted—was Billy Mulcaster.

Add it all up.

Rosie, terrified and grief-stricken, gradually forced to realize that her Billy was a crook, perhaps a killer, perhaps involved in the murder of her father. Rosie, unable to make up her mind what to do, unable to believe the shocking worst, carrying the child and living with her frightening secret; and then, under some strain which Roger didn't know about, cracking up, telephoning him, planning to tell him what she feared.

Was that it?

And had Billy suspected what she was likely to do, watched her, seen her telephone and then hurried to the main road, hustled along, fooled the policeman in the fog, forced Rosie into a side street and—left her for dead?

Roger reached the street. Traffic was at a standstill except for an occasional car, its driver persisting forlornly when the rest of London had given up hope of moving by road. The engines that were running had a strange, disembodied note. The footsteps of people walking were muffled.

A sergeant at the hospital gates said:

"Only hope is the tube, sir."

"Yes, I suppose so. I'll go to Piccadilly station and walk to Pretzel's from there," Roger said, and then suddenly changed his mind. "No, I'll go to the Yard." He walked, keeping close to the hospital wall, toward the underground station, only a few hundred yards away. Here and there, people coughed wheezily, and the fog crawled into his mouth, his eyes and nostrils, seeped into his throat. His flashlight was of little use, just threw back a pale blur; the wall was his best guide. He lost contact with it, took a step forward, and banged into a man, who said.

"Here!"

"Sorry."

"Damn curb must be somewhere."

They groped their way across. A car horn sounded, mournfully and absurdly foolish. The tall street lamps made the fog paler overhead but did not help visibility. But for the fog, Roger could have been in his office by now; and he hadn't even reached the nearest station.

If Billy Mulcaster knew that the police were really after him, he wouldn't go to the restaurant, would he? He would go to earth. Where? If he had killed O'Leary, killed others, left Rosie for dead, it hadn't been his own idea. One could believe a lot of bad things about Billy Mulcaster, but not that he was the Blower, or that he could have been the instigator of these crimes, or that he had any overwhelming motive against the Sarkeys. Only the disowned son—

Roger stopped in his tracks.

"Oh, my God," he breathed.

If they picked Billy up at Pretzel's, and if Hick was the Blower and Sarkey's real son, too, he might try to kill his father before he was trapped.

People pushed past Roger and collided with him, and grumbled. When he started to move it was to rush past everyone else. He almost fell into the gaping entrance of the underground station. Three telephone kiosks, one of them empty, were just visible through the yellow murk. He let the door bang on him, put in his three pennies and dialed Whitehall 1212.

Marino, the new waiter at the Pretzel, was very careful that night. Hick, the chef, was edgy. Everyone knew it, and was wary of him. Marino's reports to the Yard hadn't yet covered Hick in a mood like this.

The kitchen was hot, steamy, full of the smell of cooking, of spices, wines, sauces. Hick left nearly everything to his assistant, and, when the telephone bell rang, went out of the hot room to take the call upstairs.

He could switch it away from the instrument down here.

Marino, lucky because there were few diners in the restaurant, followed the big chef, whose tall hat bumped against the ceiling and nearly came off. Then Hick went into the office and slammed the door.

Marino opened it silently, taking a chance.

Hick grunted into the telephone, "Hallo, who's 'at?" and then was silent. He grunted twice again, then said, "You must be crazy, not to finish—" He stopped and then went on: "It's okay, Billy, just do what I told you."

He broke off abruptly; there was a pause. Next moment the one thing Marino really feared happened: the one thing which might drive Hick berserk. A waiter appeared at the foot of the stairs and shouted:

"Hey, you!"

Marino swung round.

Hick gasped, inside the room.

The other waiter called sarcastically, "Having a night off? Why don't you—"

Marino heard Hick's stamping footsteps. He spun round, but Hick was already at the door.

He carried a knife.

He raised it, and in his chef's hat and white clothes he looked as if he were going to carve a joint. Murder was in his eyes. He slashed at Marino, who jumped out of reach, away from the stairs. Hick turned and raced down them.

"Careful!" shouted Marino. "Look out!"

The other waiter seemed petrified. When he moved, it was a second too late. The knife sank into his flesh.

Marino, moving all the time, leaped the last few stairs. Hick hadn't time to turn round before the detective's full weight was on his back, bearing him down.

Roger heard about all this when he telephoned. There was no doubt that Billy Mulcaster had telephoned Hick, that Hick had started to bellow at him, then changed his tune and said, "Just do what I tell you."

"But Hick won't say a word; he's just like the rest," the Yard man said.

"Been to his flat yet?"

"Our men are there now. Can't move fast enough tonight, that's the trouble."

"I'll go there from here," Roger said. "Leave a message there if Mulcaster turns up."

"Okay."

"Thanks."

Roger rang off....

By tube, the journey wasn't so bad, and he walked from Piccadilly station to Hick's flat. Policemen and police cars, almost swallowed up by the fog, were outside.

Inside, it was rather as if he'd come to the end of a long journey; there was a moment of exhilaration, then a heavy, almost nagging fear because Billy Mulcaster was still at large. But not the Blower. Obviously Hick was the Blower, for in this flat, where the floorboards were up, Roger saw plastic gelignite, nitroglycerine, cordite and TNT, as well as fuses and tiny containers of nitroglycerine like the one used near the garage.

"We've got Hick for plenty," a Yard man said jubilantly.

"Any papers?" asked Roger.

"Haven't looked everywhere yet." They started to search, and ten minutes later Roger found a long, printed form: a birth certificate of Reginald Sarkey, the kind of thing he had expected, and which seemed to tell a story so plainly that it couldn't be true.

"The explosive stuff used at Sarkey's office came from here," the other Yard man said. "All the H.E. has, not much doubt of that. If anyone's wandering about with any of these little beauties in his pocket, someone could be in trouble."

illy Mulcaster was wandering about....

Barbara Denny had been kidnaped; Roger didn't yet know why, but it put her high on the danger list. Sir Gerald Sarkey had escaped murder by a fluke. Someone had been working on Sarkey's nerves for a long time, and Philip behaved as if his nerves were at breaking point.

"Time we warned the Sarkeys again, both father and son," Roger said.

"We've tried, but we can't get 'em on the telephone," the Yard man told him. "We've sent men to Parable Court, and a warning to Sunningdale, just as—"

"Sent anyone to Miss Denny's?"

"Well, no—"

"Rush someone there," Roger said tensely. "I'll go as fast as I can."

Billy Mulcaster was in fact near Wigham Street, not far from Barbara Denny's flat. He kept coughing. He kept seeing Rosie's horrified eyes as they had burned at him when he had strangled her, but he'd had to do it or she would have given him away.

He wasn't sure she was dead; not absolutely sure.

He'd felt right out on a limb, and telephoned Hick.

"Just do what I told you," Hick had said.

That should be simple.

He had talked to Hick about it earlier that afternoon. He knew exactly what he had to do to win a fortune. He had already seen plenty of money in the huge diamond ring he had given Rosie for their engagement.

Rosie—

She seemed to stare at him out of the fog.

He had to *kill* the Sarkeys.

He had already been a killer, before Hick had talked so big, saying he might as well be hanged for a sheep instead of a lamb, then patting his shoulder, smiling with that loose, damp mouth, and adding:

"But the police won't get us, Billy. I've got it all planned. There's only one man, possibly two, who could stop us now. Sarkey's my father, see. Fix both the Sarkeys and it'll mean millions, Billy, millions!"

Hick had grinned.

"Here's another little prize packet; you know what I mean." He had handed a small packet to Billy. "Take it to Barbara Denny's flat; both the Sarkeys will be there. Be careful with it. Wait until you see the two of them together. Can't be helped if the woman's there as well. Just throw the tube and get out, see. Once the door's closed you'll be okay. This is just the right night for it; no one will be able to find you.

"It'll be easier than it was at Webb Street last night, Billy, and you did that beautifully.

"And afterward we'll have millions to play with, see. *Millions!*"

Millions.

Billy Mulcaster reached the house where Barbara Denny lived. A wraithlike figure looked out of the fog: a girl.

She had Rosie's eyes.

Billy flinched.

Then he went toward the front door. It wasn't hard to force the lock. Rosie's eyes and Hick's seductive voice were everywhere; everywhere.

The tube was in his pocket.

22

One of Each

Philip Sarkey stood up from the side of the sofa where Barbara was resting, and stood looking down on her, his great head a little on one side. She looked at her regal best. Her face wasn't bruised, and the only graze was on her right temple. Her eyes were clear, although the lids looked a little heavy.

Philip stood like that for so long that she began to smile.

"What is it, Phil?"

"I was just wondering what I would have done if the worst had come to the worst," said Philip frankly. "And telling myself that reason and logic and filial duty would have tugged pretty hard, but if I'd just stood and looked at you for ten seconds —you'd have won hands down."

"Would I?"

"Yes," said Philip, "yes, you would. Even though I'd have been hellish sorry for the old man."

"I'm desperately sorry for him," Barbara said. Her eyes clouded. "Especially now. I wonder why he cut himself off from—from Reggie. You do know Reggie, don't you?"

"I hardly *know* him," said Philip, abruptly. "I've seen him a few times. I'd hardly recognize him if I saw him now. I haven't any—well, brotherly love, you know. After all, I hardly knew him when I was a kid. But I developed an unexpected bump of duty, and when he telephoned me and told me he was right up against it—well, what could I do? I squeezed him a hundred. No use asking Dad."

"But generally, Gerald's so generous," Barbara said. "Not many realize it, so few really know him. He gives away fortunes to charity, and—"

"He can afford to!"

"I wonder what made him behave as he did over me and Rosie," Barbara said, ignoring the interruption. "He'd never objected to my 'slumming' before. Something seemed to happen to him after Maitland's murder."

"It'll soon be sewn up," Philip said, almost too confidently. "That chap West hasn't done a bad job, although I could have knocked his head off when he went for Dad." Philip lit a cigarette and moved away from the couch. "Can understand him thinking White was Reggie, I suppose; he's no fool." He grinned suddenly. "I forgot—you have a soft spot for the good-looking copper, haven't you?"

"He always makes me think he'd rather help than hurt."

This was a pleasant room, with pale blue and gold the main color scheme, two delightful water colors, a little Italian enameled mirror and a few other good pieces all giving an air of elegant comfort. Barbara, in a dark blue dress, sat with her long, slim legs stretched out, a cushion at her head, her hair burnished by the subdued lights.

"I know what you mean about his eagerness to help," Philip said. Then he took the cigarette from his lips, tossed it into the coal fire, and said sharply, "Barbara, mind telling me the truth?"

"What about, Phil?"

"You. Me. Our marriage." He paused, tensely. "You don't really love me, do you? I don't make your heart beat fast, like mine beats when I see you." He stared with glistening eyes. "You don't love me like that, do you?"

Very quietly, Barbara said:

"No, Philip."

He winced, but spoke again almost at once, and very slowly.

"Thanks for being honest, anyway. Why did you say you'd marry me?"

As quietly, Barbara said:

"I was in love with someone else, Philip. He didn't respond; I don't think he even guessed. And you were so—so overwhelming. You can be, you know. We'd been such good friends, and I believed I could make you happy. That's all."

Philip twisted his lips in a tight, hurt smile.

"Do you think we could be now?"

"If you'd like to try, I'll try with you," Barbara said.

Philip brushed his hand across his eyes, lit another cigarette, went to a cocktail cabinet, and poured himself a drink. He tossed it down.

"I needed that. Well—"

He broke off, as the door opened. Letty, the maid, looked flustered. Behind her was Philip's father, tall and oddly aloof, yet with his lips touched with a smile.

"It's Sir Gerald, Miss Barbara."

"Why, Gerald!"

"Hallo, Dad, what's brought you?" Philip asked, and could not keep the hurt out of his voice.

Sarkey just smiled, but without any hint of humor. He gave the impression of being under a great strain. There was a moment or two of awkwardness, and in it the maid spoke in a subdued voice.

"Is it all right for me to go out now, Miss Barbara?"

"Yes, go along," Barbara said.

The door closed.

Sir Gerald Sarkey moved across to Barbara, leaned down, and kissed her lightly on the forehead, then turned to face his son. Barbara looked from one to the other. The sense of strain increased between these men of such sharp contrast. Philip was so much heavier, broader, massive; it was only now and again that one caught the family likeness.

"I'm very glad you're here, Philip," Sarkey said. "I wanted a few words with you both. Barbara, I'm going to explain why I didn't want you to associate with Rosie Mulcaster, or with the Mulcaster family at all." He paused, and the tension was almost unbearable. Then: "I had reason to believe that young Mulcaster might be my grandson."

He stopped.

It was as if the air had exploded.

Philip backed a pace, as if from a physical threat. Barbara closed her eyes, and when she opened them again they had a scared look.

Sarkey went on:

237

"I would like you to know, now, Philip, that for some years I endeavored to trace your brother, my elder son. It was possible that the years had changed him for the better, possible that he was worth—I dislike the word, but it is probably the only one that fits the circumstances—forgiveness. I failed to find any trace, for a long time. Then it was reported that he had changed his name to Hick, that he worked at the Pretzel Restaurant, and that his son worked there with him."

Philip said in a strangled voice, "How did you know?"

"Among the people whom a private inquiry agent in my employ interrogated was a man named O'Leary. I knew O'Leary had worked with your brother in the distant past. O'Leary told this inquiry agent about Hick. The reports on—ah—Hick's personality were not encouraging, but he appeared to be leading a reasonably industrious and honest life, and had built up an excellent reputation. I decided to have him watched and his behavior reported to me. I found out that he was still associated with O'Leary, and also with another man, named White—who is now under arrest. So I did nothing. It is true that I associated these attacks and robberies with my son at one time, but I couldn't be sure. I can't even be sure that Hick *is* Reginald. We should have a better idea in an hour's time. He is coming here tonight."

Philip cried, "*What?*"

Barbara said, "Are you—sure?"

"He telephoned me, saying that he knew I had been searching for him, that he wasn't concerned for himself but didn't see why his son—he means Mulcaster—shouldn't benefit from his—his father's good fortune. He suggested that we should meet, and that he should bring proof of his identity. I asked him to come here."

"Why here?" asked Philip. "Why *here?*"

"I wanted Barbara to be with us," Sarkey said simply.

"I don't like it at all." Philip was emphatic and agitated. "They tried to kill you this morning; who else would have done that but—but him? You're crazy to see him!"

"I don't think so, Philip. I have felt for some time that I would like to come face to face with him. Perhaps he is the murderer, perhaps he has tried to kill me. Perhaps he isn't even my son. This will be the way to find out."

"I tell you it's crazy!"

Sarkey looked at his younger son as if trying to understand this outburst. Philip colored, but didn't turn away; as the scrutiny lengthened, he said abruptly:

"What's in your mind? To give him a chance to be another prodigal son?"

Sarkey turned to Barbara.

"What do you think?" he asked.

She didn't answer, didn't even try to. She saw something in his face which told her that nothing would dissuade him. She had a strange impression that he was quite ready for death. It was a kind of fatalism. Philip was right and it was crazy; and Sarkey was right; it was like a breath of sanity stirring the arid sands of madness.

"I think you must do what you think right," she said.

"You *must* be mad!" Barbara had never heard Philip speak like that to his father, and the tightening of the older man's lips showed how much he disliked it. "I won't take chances with Barbara. He'll have to deal with me first!"

"Philip—" began Sarkey sharply.

The front-door bell rang.

Barbara caught her breath, and then said, "Letty's out. One of us—"

Philip Sarkey swung round and bounded toward the door, as if to make quite sure that his father could not get there first. He didn't look round. He pulled the door open, jumped into the hall, and slammed the door behind him.

His father stood rigid, as if he could not believe that this had happened.

"Oh, God," Barbara cried, "don't let anything happen to him, don't—"

Sarkey moved almost as swiftly as his son, reached the door, and clutched the handle. Then he heard Philip roar with a lion's rage, heard a shot, a screech—and an explosion which snatched the door out of the older man's hands, rattled pictures, and brought something heavy crashing in the hall.

23

Hick

Roger West saw the flash and heard the explosion, but couldn't do a thing about it. But for the fog, he might have been a few vital minutes earlier; and if luck had been against him, he might have been at the head of the stairs, to share the full force of the explosion with Billy Mulcaster. He felt the blast, heard the rattling pictures and a crash of something heavy falling. He went up the stairs as if his life depended on getting to the landing. Halfway up the second flight of stairs he saw what was left of Billy, and he saw another heap in the doorway. Oddly, the lion's head and the lion's mane were hardly touched. The full force of the explosion had caught Philip Sarkey in the chest; blood showed through the tattered clothes, crimsoned the white shirt.

By Philip's hand was an automatic pistol. Roger picked it up and put it in his pocket.

He heard a sound, looked up, and saw Sarkey in the other doorway, Barbara by his side.

"Get back," Roger said. "There isn't a thing you

can do." He stepped over Billy, skirted Philip, reached the doorway. Sarkey could not have stood more still if his body had turned to marble; Barbara stood in that same state of frozen immobility.

Other Yard men were coming up the stairs.

"Get back," Roger said to Sarkey and Barbara. They didn't move. "Get back and let me come in!" he roared. For the first time they seemed to see and to hear him, but he had to take the man's arm and force him into the room. He kicked the door to, cutting off the sight on the landing. "Listen," he said. "A man claiming to be your other son now calls himself Hick; he runs the Pretzel Restaurant; he sent Billy Mulcaster to kill both of you. I don't know whether he's your son or not. I just know that Philip took the brunt. Understand that? Philip died to save you."

Sarkey closed his eyes.

"I think I understand," Barbara said in a tired voice. "I think Sir Gerald will, too. You're very good." She was beginning to feel again, and Roger saw her sway. There was no one here to help where help was desperately needed.

"Philip—Philip tried to save him," Barbara went on, in that deliberate, emphatic voice. "Philip—tried—"

"One good, one bad," Roger said, "and Sir Gerald wasn't responsible for either; they just came that way. Make him understand."

"I—I'll try." Barbara swayed and Roger grabbed her. He helped her to the couch, then turned and looked at Sarkey, who hadn't moved. He had never seen a man who looked so awfully alone. He wondered if a single friend could help him, if a single soul would really try.

And then he saw a wondrous thing.

"Gerald," said Barbara, in a different voice, a voice which had warmth and longing in it, spoken with great distress but unmistakable meaning. "Gerald, please, don't stand there like that. Come to me."

Sir Gerald Sarkey heard her, raised his head slowly, and for a moment kept completely still. Slowly the severe lines of his face, the lines of shock, began to soften. He moved, faltering, but he moved with both arms outstretched. She held her good arm toward him. Roger saw the look in her eyes which, in precious moments, he saw in Janet's.

He turned away, a savage movement, and went out, leaving them together.

Life would stop for Sir Gerald Sarkey if Hick was his son; and begin for them both if he was not.

Turnbull was superintending the routine work on the landing. He was the only one of the detectives who looked his normal color, and even his voice lacked its usual brashness.

"How's the cold fish?" he asked, straightening up from Philip's body. "On top of his own little world, as usual?"

"No," said Roger. "We were wrong. He is human."

"Poor devil," said Turnbull. "Still, fifty-fifty, one good, one bad. Most parents have that kind of brood even if they don't run to extremes." He looked almost embarrassed at that lapse into sentiment. "Except for Handsome West, of course!"

Roger found a grin.

"If Hick's the real son," he said. "We haven't proof, yet. I'm going to see Hick." He nodded and started down the stairs. Turnbull and the others paused in their task to look at him.

Hick was in the charge room at the Yard, wearing a big shapeless overcoat over his white smock, a faint aroma of garlic and spices about him. His loose mouth was set more tightly than usual, and his hooded eyes seemed brighter, as if he knew that he had reached the end.

A uniformed sergeant and a constable were with him.

"Wait outside a minute, will you?" Roger asked them, and they didn't argue.

"Well, Hick," Roger said, "we've got you."

"That so?" It was little more than a grunt.

"We found enough stuff at your flat to hang you," Roger said. "You can make it hard for us and hard for yourself, or you can make it easy. I want the truth. I'm alone, with no witness, so I can't use what you say in evidence. If I tried, I'd have every self-righteous defense counsel and every high-minded M.P. screaming blue murder. So this is off the record."

Hick looked at him, eyes hooded.

"Was Mulcaster really your son?"

Hick didn't answer.

"You sent him to kill and to die. We know exactly what you meant on the telephone," Roger said. "Was he your son?"

Hick's drooping lids covered his eyes except for two bright, narrow slits.

"Hard or easy, it doesn't make any difference to me," Roger said, "but where will the hard way get you? It's only a matter of time before we find out, so why not tell me now?"

"Why don't you find things out for yourself?" Hick sneered.

"All right, let's see how far I've got," Roger said briskly, and schooled himself not to show how much Hick's reaction could mean. He knew a great deal that could be proved; he suspected other vital things which he might never be able to prove if Hick refused to talk. "You are not Sarkey's son; you only pretended to be. We can come to the reason for that later. Your connection with the family was through the second son, Philip." Roger paused just long enough to see that startle Hick before he went on. "We can dig pretty deep at the Yard. We dug until we found out that, in his early motor-racing days, Philip needed a lot more money than his father allowed him. So he began to take jewelry from Jefferson's, and to sell it. That's probably how he came to know you and White—you bought some of the stuff and saw a chance to make a big thing out of Philip. You developed your working plan. Philip told you the best times to raid the different stores, and you raided with the Gelignite Gang. Having inside knowledge made it much easier for you, and Philip's cut was big enough to keep him happy."

Roger paused for a moment, and then flashed:

"Isn't that true?"

Hick's eyes betrayed him, plainly showing astonishment, but he didn't answer.

Roger felt the rising tide of elation.

"You had everything working smoothly, and Philip where you wanted him," he went on. "You had his father harassed and hounded by the fear that his first son was taking revenge. The setup looked perfect, but you knew that it couldn't last, that if you went on too long, you and the gang would be caught. Before that happened you wanted to make a final killing, and it had to be big. Not just another robbery, but something to bring in millions. How's that, Hick?"

Hick stood very still.

"Sir Gerald Sarkey had the millions you were after," Roger went on, "and you tried to cover yourself so that if one way of getting them failed, you'd switch to another. You could kill Sir Gerald and squeeze Philip, but if that didn't work and both Sarkeys had to be killed you could put Billy Mulcaster up as the grandson. We found birth certificates at your flat which told us part of this story."

Hick moved, as if he didn't like the strain, but he made no admission and no denial.

"You had to have Mulcaster under your thumb, too, and that wasn't difficult," Roger continued, more briskly. "Mulcaster's first job was to work on old Maitland, and he started through Maitland's daughter. You hadn't bargained for love and a marriage but it made no material difference. When you thought the time had come, you carried out the raid. You'd bribed the other night watchman to keep Maitland upstairs, but when he came downstairs he had to be killed. That wasn't simply to stop him from raising the alarm," Roger asserted confidently. "That was chiefly because he might have recognized Billy. O'Leary knew that when he struck Maitland; the only safe Maitland was a dead one.

"Only it didn't work out that way," Roger said

grimly. "The murder worked on Mulcaster's nerves so badly that you had to put O'Leary onto the job of watching him. But Mulcaster was tougher than you'd realized, and when he was in a tight corner, he killed O'Leary. That right?"

He snapped out the last words.

Hick was beginning to wilt; his shoulders drooped, and he looked as if he was very tired. He moistened his lips and then broke his long silence.

"Yeh," he said huskily. "Yeh, that's how it was."

For Roger, it was like being on top of the world, but his voice and expression didn't betray his elation.

"Mulcaster in his tough mood might have been dangerous to you," he went on briskly, "but you quieted him down with talk of the Sarkey millions. You might have been all right for a while, but for the consequences of the other revolt—Philip Sarkey's. Philip wouldn't stand for the murder, and was sick of being made to do whatever you wanted. You had to stop him, so—"

Hick raised one hand. "West, how—how did you get onto Philip Sarkey? I can't see—" He broke off, as if bewildered.

"There had to be a motive for kidnaping Barbara Denny," Roger said, almost offhandedly, "and while I was looking for that motive I considered Philip. He nearly went mad when he heard that the woman was kidnaped; in fact he was so distraught that he seemed almost to blame himself. It didn't take long to see that he'd been living on his nerves for a long time, too. Measure those things against the fact that the Gelignite Gang invariably knew when to raid a store, which suggested inside help, and we had a new line to follow. The case against Philip Sarkey built up from there, starting with the possibility Miss Denny might have been kidnaped in order to increase pressure on Philip See how it was done?"

"I get it," Hick muttered. "One of these days you'll put two and two together and make five."

"We can always take one away," Roger said blandly. "One of the things you people don't realize is that we never stop looking, and that we've learned to recognize pieces that fit. Here's another The brakes in Miss Denny's car, which toppled into the water at Tivvy Docks, had been fixed so that the driver couldn't stop at the edge. That kept him quiet, and if you'd had the luck, the car would have been hidden under water for the night. But your luck was running out at the same time as White's. White kidnaped Miss Denny and took her away in the Packard, but some mechanics were working late at the Webb Street garage so he had to drive away, park the car in a yard where Miss Denny wouldn't be seen, leave her bound and gagged, and wait until he could get into the garage. When we raided the garage, he called you. You sent the car loaded with nitroglycerine, but that didn't come off either."

Hick looked as if the relentless recital was too much for him. Roger felt the full excitement of elation, almost sure that Hick would talk.

"Let's have the rest," he said abruptly. "You're not Sarkey's son, and Mulcaster isn't your son."

"Okay, West," Hick said in a tired voice, "you can have it all. You're right, too, it started when young Sarkey sold some of Jefferson's stuff, and White and me got onto it. White was a pal of that older son of Sarkey, Reggie. He died in an air raid, did you know?" That wasn't a gibe, just a flat, dispirited question. "We thought we might be able to squeeze a bit out of the old man, but it didn't come to anything. Then Philip came along, and it all began to build up. The mistake I made was trying to pass off Billy Mulcaster as Sarkey's grandson. It looked good when I started, but—" Hick broke off, scowling as if at his own folly. "So it didn't come off."

"We'll have all this drawn up in the form of a statement," Roger said, "and you can check it and sign it tomorrow." Hick didn't argue. "Fill in a few more details first, will you? How did you dispose of the jewelry you took from Jefferson's?"

"Sold most of it back to a different branch from where we took it," Hick said. "O'Leary was a silversmith and jeweler, see. He altered the stuff, changed the marks, and cut up all the big stones; good commercial job he did. Philip Sarkey told the department buyers to patronize Dillon and White when they called, so it was easy."

Too easy.

"Thanks. Another thing—why did Dillon run wild?"

"He always was a risk," Hick said gruffly. "He killed a man about six years ago, and never could keep his head. Coppers scared him. Pal o' White's, Dillon was; if it hadn't been for that I wouldn't have had any truck with him."

"Hmm." Roger paused, and then added as if absently, "Did you seriously think you might be able to pass Mulcaster off as Sarkey's grandson?"

"There was a good chance," Hick said with quiet certainty. "His son Reggie had a kid, see, about the same age as Billy Mulcaster. The kid was killed in an air raid. It was chiefly a question of switching identity documents—that's been done before—and fixing a few witnesses. But you know the chances as well as I do, West."

"Fifty-fifty, I suppose," conceded West, musingly. He was quiet for a moment, then asked with the familiar deceptive casualness, "Why did you try to kill Sir Gerald the other night? Did you think that Philip would stand for that?"

"If Mr. Ruddy Philip hadn't, we would have put him away too, then worked on the grandson angle," Hick said. He stared into Roger's eyes and gave a quick, wry grin as he added steadily, "Like to know the whole truth, West? You and the Yard was too good for us, that's what. Didn't give us any breathing space once you got on the Maitland job, and you pushed us into making mistakes. When we started the game, it looked as if it couldn't miss."

"I can believe that," Roger said dryly.

He sent for a sergeant to take Hick away, and then began to prepare the statement which Hick was to sign. Hick would probably argue that he hadn't said this thing or the other, but in the long run he would sign, because life would be much easier if he was co-operative.

It was over, bar the shouting.

And bar the pain and the suffering that were stored up for Sir Gerald Sarkey. His first son wholly bad, his second weak and corrupted, betraying Jefferson's and the great organization which his father had built up.

There was just one thing that might help Sarkey: the knowledge that Philip had died while trying to make amends.

Could Sarkey be made to realize that was true?

On the day that Hick and White were hanged at Wandsworth Jail, Roger West left Scotland Yard in the middle of the morning and went to Oxford Street. He didn't have to wait long for a lift, and was taken straight up to Sarkey's office. The secretary's door was opened by Rosie Mulcaster, any man's dream in black and white.

"Good morning, Rosie."

She smiled, obviously pleased to see him. "Good morning, Mr. West. I'll tell Sir Gerald you're here." She picked up the telephone and spoke, then smiled again. "Please go straight in."

Roger went in.

Sir Gerald Sarkey was already rounding his desk to greet him. Barbara was getting up from her chair.

"Very good of you to come," Sarkey said. "We've all been living very much in the past this morning. Did everything—" He paused.

"Everything went off according to plan," Roger told him, "and I wanted to tell you that myself."

"Just as you told me that Philip saved my life by deliberately risking his own," Sarkey said; and obviously there was peace in him. After a pause, he went on: "You know people, don't you, West? Rubbing shoulders with so many criminals hasn't really hardened you."

"The difficulty is judging when to be tough," Roger said dryly. "Don't you agree, Lady Sarkey?"

He had always liked Barbara's smile....

Roger didn't go to the Yard, but drove to Bell Street, arriving a little after twelve. The boys would soon be home for the midday meal. He opened the front door and tiptoed to the kitchen. Janet, her back toward him, was poking a fork into something in a saucepan.

"*Boo!*" squeaked Roger.

Janet jumped round. "Martin, don't—oh, you *fool!*" She broke into a laugh, and then made a face at him. "You get more like a boy every day. Can you stay for lunch?"

"Lunch, tea, dinner, a theater—"

"You mean you've a day *off?*"

"Yes, ma'am!"

"Oh, that's wonderful! Darling, be a pet and go and start laying the table for me. The boys want to leave at one fifteen sharp; their class is going to visit the British Museum or Madame Tussaud's or somewhere this afternoon. Lay for five."

"Five?"

"Peter Smith is coming," Janet said. "Martin's protégé, remember? If you were ever here you'd know that Peter is always in and out; he makes this his home away from home. And he *washes*. In fact the only thing he gets wrong now," Janet added, smiling almost too brightly, "is the notion that Martin and Richard have a father to be proud of."

"Peculiar idea," Roger agreed solemnly. "All right, I'll lay the table."

He went out, whistling, opened the wrong cupboard in the sideboard, and saw a half-full bottle of whisky which Janet had shrewdly tucked away. He grinned, found a glass, poured himself a finger, splashed in soda, and then began to do his chores.